Veering From the Straight and Narrow

by
Paul Magnan

1

ISBN: 978-1792872280
ISBN-10: 1792872283

Table of Contents

The Heart of Hell

Had he spoken the right words? Had anything been forgotten?
Gary looked up from the thin book. The old leather cover felt
brittle in his hands. There was nothing in the basement besides
himself and the circled pentagram he had drawn with white
chalk on the cement floor. There was a chill in the air, but it was
always colder down here than in the rest of the house. He stood
and waited a few minutes more. Nothing happened.

He considered reciting the incantation again. With a sigh he
closed the book. It had taken him seven months to find it, and
$600 to purchase it. A fool and his money…

Gary stepped outside of the circle and paused. Nothing. Not
even a trickle of a breeze. He looked around one last time and
walked up the stairs.

In his bedroom Gary turned on his old desktop computer. He
had considered getting a laptop, or even one of those "smart"
phones, but he kept to what he knew he could use. Truth be told,
he was intimidated by how quickly computer technology
continued to change. Something that was state of the art in the
morning was considered hopelessly obsolete by dinnertime.
Who could keep up with that? No, Gary was fine staying with
what he knew, at least until the old computer broke down for
good and he was forced to deal with something new.

A minute later he was on the Internet, searching through the
matchmaker and singles sites which, if they were books, would
be well-thumbed. Photos of beautiful models with hollow smiles

greeted him, with taglines like *Ashley is waiting to hear from you!* Gary knew full well Ashley was not waiting to hear from him. Most people who used these sites did so out of desperation, submitting pictures of themselves when they were ten years younger and forty pounds lighter. The few times Gary had tried to make a connection ended up being disasters. Tentative on-line greetings followed by awkward face-to-face encounters, with polite, meaningless conversations that did not hide the disappointment both sides felt. They ended with promises to stay in touch that neither side intended to keep.

Gary wasn't bad looking. At forty-two, he was still in decent shape. His dark hair was turning gray, but not enough to make him look older than what he was. Physically, he could still catch the eyes of pretty women.

But when they got close, they got a whiff of his neediness and fled like pigeons from a circling hawk.

Gary shut down the computer and went to the double bed he had to himself.

\#

She had dark hair, long and shiny like the hair the models had in those glossy magazines. Her skin was dark, but not any color from the race of man. It was deep red, like blood fresh from the heart. Her eyes were bright and full of desire, with irises the orange of a bloated moon. Two nubs protruded from her forehead, too small and delicate to be called horns.

Her smile broke through the barriers surrounding his heart. Her hand caressed his bare chest. Long black nails, sharp as talons, tickled his skin before they withdrew.

"Gary," she whispered, the word encompassing him and nobody else. "I am here for you. You are no longer alone. All you have to do is accept me." Her black eyebrows rose and her glistening lips puckered in a way that was adorable and irresistible. "Do you accept me, Gary?"

She was in his arms. Her body was warm and felt perfect. It was what he had been waiting for his entire life.

"Who are you?" he asked. "What's your name?"

She pulled his head down and her lips brushed his ear. "Lissa."

Yearning flooded through him. He wanted Lissa. He needed her. But he had to know.

"Are you the one I summoned?"

"Yes, and I'm so glad you did. Now we're here for each other."

Gary closed his eyes. "For how long?"

Lissa pressed a finger to his lips. "Shhh. That part's a long time away. And it won't be so bad. I'll still be with you. We'll be together forever."

Lissa pressed her lips to his. Gary's body tingled. Her hand lowered, and her fingers teased his growing erection.

"Do you accept?"

Gary had trouble catching his breath, but he finally managed to exhale. "Yes."

#

Gary popped awake and sat up. Early morning light crept through the drawn shade of the window. He ran a hand through his hair. The vividness of the dream had been incredible. He could still taste those lips. *Lissa...*

7

A long nail trailed down his bare arm.

Gary screamed and jumped out of bed. He looked without comprehension at the red-skinned, orange-eyed woman who lounged naked on the other side of the bed.

"Hello, dear," the strange woman purred. She looked to the window. "It looks like it's going to be a beautiful day. We can go out and enjoy it later." She patted Gary's vacated space on the bed. "How about we have some fun first?"

Gary shook his head, unable to believe what he was seeing. "You're the one from my dream."

"Yes."

"How is it you're real? Dreams don't come to life."

Lissa stretched out on the bed, the muscles underneath her skin rippling in a way that drew Gary's desire to the forefront. Her body was beyond fantastic.

"Sure they do. All you have to do is accept."

Do you accept?

He remembered the question from his dream. He had said yes.

Gary turned to the book, which lay next to his computer. Why not believe this was true? It was what he had tried to accomplish, after all. It just came about in a way he hadn't expected.

His heartbeat quickened. "You're real."

Laughter came from his bed, delighted and intimate. "Of course I am."

Gary turned to Lissa. "How long do I have with you before...?"

Lissa rose from the bed and wrapped her arms around Gary's neck. "Let's not worry about that. We'll have all sorts of time. Besides, didn't I already say we would still be together?"

"Yeah, but that's where you come from. Of course you would be there."

"With you," Lissa emphasized with a lingering kiss. Gary's embraced her. He did not want the kiss to stop.

Lissa pulled away, and he reluctantly let her do so. Her smile was warm and inviting and for him alone. "Who would you like for me to be?"

"What do you mean?"

"I can be anyone you want me to be. Anyone you have ever fantasized about. I can be the girl you had a crush on in high school."

Lissa's body morphed into Christine Bannon, at the age he remembered her when they graduated twenty-four years ago. Like Lissa she was nude, and Gary was willing to bet all the anatomical features were correct.

"Or how about the actress whose pictures you're always downloading?"

The blonde, slim teenager changed into the raven-haired movie star whom Gary had admired since her television beginnings.

"I can even be that cute young thing who runs the cashier at the grocery store."

Lissa became Becky from the Food Mart.

"I can be anyone you want me to be, a different person every night if you'd like."

Gary took a step back and gathered his racing thoughts. Somehow, Lissa knew everyone he had ever lusted after. It was scary. He felt violated... but also a little excited. The possibilities were beyond imagination. Yet...

"I think I would like it if you were just you."

Lissa changed back to her natural form. Her orange eyes were quizzical. "Are you sure?"

Despite the variety offered, this was what he wanted. "Yes."

Lissa paused, as if at a loss for words. She smiled, and Gary thought he saw a slight hint of sincerity. "Okay. That works for me."

Gary took her hand and led her back to the bed. "It works for me, too."

#

Two days later Gary announced he was wrung dry and wanted to go out and take a walk. Lissa changed her appearance enough to deflect attention while still looking reasonably like herself. She created a pair of shorts, along with sneakers and a loose cotton top.

They walked through a park near Gary's home. The path was shaded by fresh green leaves from elm and maple trees. Squirrels chittered back and forth as they raced up tree trunks and along high, winding branches. They took their time and held hands, and greeted others who were taking advantage of the sun-drenched day. Gary felt miraculously normal, like he finally belonged to the exclusive club of ordinary human existence.

Lissa chatted and pointed at things around her. She never stopped smiling and often leaned against Gary as they walked.

He squeezed her hand. "Tell me about yourself. What do you like to do?"

"I like being with you."

"Thank you, but don't you have other interests?"

Lissa stopped. "What other interests can I have? Gary, I'm here for you. No other reason."

"I know, but," Gary floundered a bit, looking for the right words. "Even beyond me, you are a distinctive personality. How did you come to be? What did you do before you came here?"

Lissa's face clouded over, becoming its natural blood-red color. "You don't want to know any of that, Gary. It's not important. I don't want to talk about it. All that matters is being here with you."

"Well, it seems to me, our time here is limited. Once we go back to where you come from, I'd like to know how you tick, so I..."

"No!" Lissa backed away. Her irises went from brown to orange. "This is not to be discussed. Not ever. Why can't you just accept me in the here and now?"

Gary felt lost. How could he explain to Lissa his desire to know these things without upsetting her further? "Lissa, I'm sorry, but this is what couples do. They get to know each other. You already seem to know everything about me, but I know nothing about you. I want to know who you are, underneath everything else."

Lissa shook her head. "No. You're asking for what I can't give you."

"Why not?"

Sudden heat radiated from Lissa's body. Long black nails grew from her fingers. Her eyes became solid ebony.

"Because I can't!" Lissa yelled. "It's not allowed. Can't you get that through your damned head?"

Lissa disappeared.

"Lissa!" Gary ran forward to the empty space where she had stood. He looked around. She was gone.

Stupid! You stupid idiot! You couldn't keep your mouth shut, and now she's gone.

Holding back tears, Gary turned and started the long walk home.

#

Lissa was in the bedroom, sitting on the bed.

"Lissa! Oh, thank God you're still here."

"Don't thank God, Gary. He has nothing to do with it."

"Sorry. Figure of speech." Gary sat on the bed next to Lissa. She didn't move, but would not look at him. They sat in silence as he struggled to come up with words to make things right.

"I'm sorry," he said. "I didn't mean to upset you. I keep forgetting that this situation is not... an average thing. I realize that you're here because of what I did, and that I have to pay a price at the end. It's just that you make me feel so good. I haven't felt this way since... well, ever. Maybe I'm reading too much into this. Maybe you're just really good at pretending you like me. But I do like you. A lot. And I guess... I guess I just want to share my happiness with you. I want you to enjoy this, too. But I'm not sure you can. Still, if there's any chance that you can feel even a bit like I do, I'll do what I can to help that along."

Lissa remained silent. Gary sighed and looked away. "I'm sorry I tried to pry into who you are. It's just that I want to get to know you, the real you, but if this upsets you, then I won't push it. I'll accept whatever you decide to give me and be glad for it."

Lissa sat as if made of stone.

Gary got up. "I'll leave you alone." He walked to the bedroom door.

"It's okay."

He stopped and turned to Lissa. She gave him a gentle, pensive smile.

"I didn't mean to get mad at you," she said. "It wasn't your fault. It's just that there are certain things I cannot talk about, such as what I am and where I come from. It's not allowed. I…" Lissa looked away. "I could be punished if I talk about it."

Gary's heart tore in his chest. "Lissa, I'm so sorry. I would never want to get you in trouble. I'll never bring it up again."

Her smile brightened and she got up from the bed. "It's okay, Gary. No harm done." She walked to him and rested her hands on his shoulders. "And yes, I do like you. I don't have to pretend with you. You are sweet and decent." Lissa reached up and gave him a tender kiss. "You think I know everything about you, but that knowledge is narrow. I can see your sexual desires, but that's it. Everything else about you," Lissa paused and kissed him again. "I'd like to find out."

#

The months went by and Gary imprinted every moment with Lissa into his memory. The bicycle rides, the walks, the museums, the concerts, every single meal, were shared with intensifying intimacy.

Gary stared into Lissa's orange eyes as he climaxed, his arms wrapped around her nude body as she kissed him. He ran his fingers through her sweat-drenched hair and put his lips to her ear.

"I love you, Lissa. You mean everything to me."

Hot tears fell on Gary's face as Lissa sobbed and held him tight.

\#

A week before the one year anniversary of Lissa entering his life, Gary found her once again sitting on the bed. Tears streamed down her face, and she pointedly refused to look at him.

Gary's heart sank. Consciously he could not put words to it, but down where it mattered he knew what she was thinking.

He tried to swallow the lump in his throat. "It's almost time, isn't it?"

Lissa did not answer.

Gary stood there and felt awful. He didn't know what else to say.

"I messed up." Her words came out as a soft exhalation.

Gary wasn't sure he heard her correctly. "What do you mean?"

"I messed up," Lissa repeated. "I know better. I've done this before. But this time," She looked up at Gary. "This time, you made it different."

Gary wanted to reach out to Lissa, but he held back. "How did I make it different?"

"Everyone else who summons me say they want a companion, but really all they want is sex. But not with me. They want sex with those they know they can never have sex with. Movie stars. Rock stars. Models. Attractive girls they knew in school. Attractive women they know at work. Any good-looking piece of tail that catches their eye."

More tears welled in Lissa's eyes.

"But not you. You wanted *me*. Not only to have sex with, but to know, and to love. You have an idea of what I am and where I'm from. You know that there will be a terrible price to pay at the end, yet you took every measure you could to not only maximize your fulfillment, but mine as well. But I'm not supposed to feel fulfillment. That's not why I'm here."

Gary kept quiet. He knew any words from him would be a mistake.

Lissa sighed. "I'm from a world that has no love, or joy, or fulfillment. Pain and suffering are the only coin there. Creatures like me are created to entice mortals to willingly give their souls to feed that vast, ravenous place. It's so easy. Mortals don't, they can't, comprehend what they will face, how horrible it will be. They live in an existence that, even if their lives are miserable, eventually comes to an end. They can't understand any other concept. But when their time with me is up, they go to a place where there is no end, or any hope of change or relief or respite."

Lissa closed her eyes and sobbed harder. "This is where you are going in a week. And when I said I was going with you, I wasn't telling the whole truth. Yes, I am going back, but I won't be with you. You will be all alone, forever. We will never be together again."

Coldness deeper than arctic ice seeped into Gary. "What will happen to you?"

Lissa looked away. "Your first concern is still about me, even though it is because of me that you will suffer for eternity."

"Lissa," Gary whispered. "This past year has been the best of my life. Whatever happens, I will always have it. In my heart, I will always have you. I have no regrets. Please, tell me, what will happen to you?"

Lissa seemed to come to a decision. She rose from the bed and wrapped her arms around Gary and rested her head on his chest.

15

"You have changed me, Gary, in a way that is anathema to my kind. My sole reason for being is manipulation. Love and caring do not factor into it. But somehow you reversed that. You made me into something I was never meant to be."

She lifted her head from his chest and looked at him. "You ask what will happen to me when I go back. I will be destroyed."

Gary recoiled. "No!"

Lissa put a finger to Gary's lips. "Yes. To those who created me, I have been compromised beyond use. I now feel care, and empathy, and love. I cannot function as I was meant to any longer. That will not be tolerated."

Gary refused to believe it. "Do you have to go back? Can't you stay here?"

"No. I have no choice but to go back. Besides, why would I remain here without you? There would be nothing for me here. It is better to be destroyed."

Tears sprang from Gary's eyes. "Lissa, I'm so sorry…"

"No," Lissa said firmly. "Do not be sorry. I am grateful to you. You have given me something I was never meant to have. You have given me the beauty and goodness, the wondrousness and happiness that is possible in existence. I have changed for the better. And it's all because of you." She reached up and kissed him. "You say you have no regrets. I do, for what will happen to you. I have no regrets for myself. I will go to my doom glad of what I have become. Thank you, Gary."

No more words would come to either of them. They held each other long into the night.

#

In the basement where, exactly one year previously, Gary had read a few lines from a thin book, he now stood and held the hand of the infernal creature he had summoned and had come to love.

The circled pentagram had faded a bit but was still legible. Now he stood outside it. It would not protect him. He had a debt to pay.

Gary thought he smelled something burning upstairs. Not that it mattered now.

The exact one year mark was five minutes away. Gary was terrified, but as he looked at Lissa, at her dark red skin, her orange eyes, and the horn-like nubs on her forehead, he knew he would have changed nothing.

Lissa turned and took Gary's other hand. Her eyes misted and she smiled. "I love you."

Gary's grip tightened on hers. "I love you, too."

The light in the cellar dimmed. A darkness that smelled of rot and fire swirled around them, enclosing them, separating them from the year of bliss they had shared.

"Kiss me," Lissa whispered.

Gary bent his neck and his lips melded with Lissa's.

Every conscious thought was sucked out of his mind and into Lissa. Gary was emptied of everything that made him who he was. He tried to pull away but Lissa held him firm. Memories and desires, his very individuality, was drawn out of him and into her.

The darkness opened, revealing despair and torment on a scale Gary could not begin to understand, where nothing existed except absolute hopelessness and loss.

Lissa broke the kiss. She wore his features. She had his body. She looked at him with his eyes and smiled sadly in a reflection of his own personality.

She pushed him into the center of the pentagram. He tried to speak, to even gather a thought, and could not. He couldn't even remember his name.

"Goodbye," she said in a male voice he thought he should recognize. Then the thing that looked like a man, but wasn't, was pulled into endless blackness…

\#

He woke on a cold cement floor, inside a circled star drawn from chalk. He shook his head and wondered what he was doing there. He also wondered who he was.

He walked up the stairs and entered a kitchen that was vaguely familiar. He knew this house, didn't he? It seemed he did, but it wasn't quite clicking in yet. He went to the sink and saw a pile of ashes. He pulled out a small piece that had not burned, a fragment of an old leather cover from some sort of book. He dropped it back into the sink.

He looked to the table where a single sheet of paper lay. He picked it up and read the brief note written on it:

If you are reading this then you are safe. Within a day you will remember everything. I am gone, forever, but I have taken with me more than what I came with. Thank you, my love.

Though he did not understand why, tears fell from his eyes. It just felt right.

Hatchlings

Sarah sipped her coffee and rolled up her sleeves. She flicked back the hasp on the window over the kitchen sink and pulled up the glass pane. The warm spring breeze kissed her skin like a long-absent lover. Outside, the birds trilled and newborn greenery shot up from the ground. The scent of thawed earth held the promise of ripe tomatoes and juicy watermelons.

Sarah smiled at the noise of children in the yard. Her two boys, Kevin and Kurt, had been indoors for most of the winter, leaving the house only to go to school. Video games had kept them occupied for a time, but the natural element for a six- and eight-year-old was outdoors. Now they were free to shed their pent-up energy to the endless blue sky.

She looked out at the vast expanse of her yard, several acres of property surrounded on three sides by forest land, with the front opening up to the road. Sarah and her husband Mitch had bought this house ten years earlier, before the boys had come along. Maintaining everything was a lot of work, especially with Mitch traveling so much with his job as a supply chain consultant, but for Sarah it was a dream come true.

The raucous laughter of the boys drifted further away. They had been told that the forest was off-limits. But of course, they pushed this boundary, especially after being kept inside all winter.

Well, it's a nice day for a walk in the yard anyway. Sarah didn't think she would need a jacket. She walked outside and sunlight tickled her skin. Mild spring air welcomed her in its embrace. She inhaled deeply and held the fresh air in her lungs for as long as she could. She smiled, exhaled slowly, and went looking for her two errant boys.

She knew where they were headed. The old, massive oak tree was on the northwest edge of their property, and it was a favorite place for the boys to look for insects.

The tree came into view almost immediately: the bark on its huge, lumpy trunk was thick and grooved, with tight, brown tendrils of creeper vine snaking around it. The gnarled branches, some with brown leaves still clinging stubbornly to them, twisted toward the sky, pushing aside smaller, lesser trees.

Kevin and Kurt had their backs to her. The mid-morning sun was bright on them, illuminating every strand of the light brown hair they had inherited from Sarah.

Something had their attention. Kevin, the oldest, had his magnifying glass. The two boys were surrounded by dozens of flying insects, thin and wispy, with large, fluttering wings. Were the mayflies out already?

Sarah stepped closer and saw that Kevin had the magnifying glass trained on an opening within the bore of the oak, where the insects streamed from.

A tiny white circle danced around the opening, expanding and contracting with the movement of the lens. One winged creature crawled into the light. It curled and started to smoke. Sarah saw the charred remains of five or six others in the same area. The boys giggled as the insect blackened and shrank.

Anger flashed through her. "Give me that!" she said, snatching the magnifying glass from Kevin's hand. "How would you like it if someone did that to you? Get back to the house right now!"

The boys moaned but turned and walked back toward the house.

The insects flew around Sarah's head with a tinny buzzing sound. One landed on the sleeve of her blouse. Sarah looked at it to make sure it wouldn't sting her.

She noticed it had four limbs instead of six. It was pale and hairless and looked at her with rage-filled eyes that were shockingly human.

Sarah gasped and looked around. Tiny, naked human forms, male and female, zipped around her with wide wings. Their mouths were open; the tinny buzzing sounds were their screams of fury. She looked back at the hole in the tree, at the charred corpses, and noticed human-like arms and legs twisted in agonized death.

Something stung her arm. A thin splinter stuck in her skin. She saw a tiny flying human figure fit another arrow in a small bow.

Painful stings peppered Sarah's arms and face. At least fifty of the creatures were shooting arrows at her. Dozens of miniature arrows buried themselves in her hair. She ran for the house. The creatures swarmed and followed. She caught up with the boys, who were walking morosely.

"Run! Get in the house now!"

The boys turned and saw the creatures chasing their mother. Eyes wide, they bolted for the door of the house, reaching it ahead of Sarah.

Sarah ran in after them and slammed the screen door shut. Hundreds of tiny flying humans grasped the mesh and spat through the screen. Many of them checked the edges for an opening wide enough to admit them.

She slammed shut the main door.

Sarah turned to the window over the sink. It was nearly black with miniscule faces twisted in fury. Tiny fists pounded the

21

screen, and a few used metallic slivers as swords to try to cut through the screen. Sarah pulled down the windowpane and locked it in place.

She winced as she pulled out a few of the arrows, each raising a drop of blood as it was drawn from her skin. It would take hours to pull them all out. She would be a mess. Thankfully the two boys had left before the arrow attack. Sarah would examine them, anyway. The arrows were easy to miss, and if left in could cause an infection.

She picked up the phone. "Hello, Stevens Pest Control? This is Sarah Wright, at 153 Faoil Lane. It seems I have a wood sprite infestation. Yes, it's pretty bad. Can you send an exterminator today? Thank you."

Wedding Day

Ellen and I climbed the short flight of stairs to the upper level of my raised ranch home. She wore the simple white dress from the ceremony, her blonde hair tumbling down the back in ringlets and waves. She looked back at me with hazel eyes that sparkled along with her smile. I carried an overnight bag that contained her clothes for the next day. Ellen was planning on moving the rest of her stuff out of her apartment tomorrow.

We walked with anticipation down the carpeted hall to the master bedroom. I opened the door and ushered Ellen in. The queen-sized bed was made, with a pastel green cover spread taut over the mattress and pillows.

Ellen did a little twirl on the toes of her white shoes. Then she smiled and flopped like a bag of flour across the foot of the bed.

I applauded her impromptu dance number.

"That was act one," Ellen said as she stood. "Now for act two."

Muted afternoon light filtered through the drawn curtains of the window. It bathed Ellen in a perfect golden radiance as she slipped out of the dress.

I stood motionless as she approached me. Her light fingers stripped off my wedding clothes. Once I was down to my skin we embraced. Ellen's lips fused with mine. She gave her entire mouth to me in a kiss that encompassed earthly bliss, then took my hands and pulled me toward the bed.

"Ellen," I said. "Now that we're married, there's something you need to see."

My new wife smiled. "Show me tomorrow."

I pulled my hands away. "No. I have to show you now." I gestured to a door to the left of the bed.

Ellen's face tightened. "What's so important about a closet?"

"That's not a closet. That's a room you haven't seen yet."

Interest sparked in her eyes, but she was pissed at me for breaking the mood. "Are you sure this can't wait until tomorrow?"

"I'm very sure. Please, this will just take a minute."

Ellen shook her head and rolled off the bed from the far side. "Well, if we're going to do this, let's get it done."

I opened the door. The room on the other side was small, barely larger than the closet Ellen had supposed it to be. A red wooden box, three feet square, sat by itself in a corner.

Ellen was unimpressed. "This is what you wanted me to see?"

I went up to the red box and waved Ellen forward. "I couldn't show you before our wedding vows, but now I can."

Ellen sighed. "Just show me already."

I grasped the hinged lid and pulled it up.

Seven black, multi-jointed legs clawed their way out of the box. They skittered down the side and hit the hardwood floor with a clatter. The legs flexed, and the rest of the creature emerged.

It was black, with a compact, bulbous body and a hairless head. Its face, twisted with hunger, was human. It was an exact duplicate of my own.

Its eyes locked on my wife.

Ellen screamed and ran for the door.

Three of the creature's spidery limbs shot out and wrapped around Ellen's legs. She dropped to the floor. She reached in desperation for the door frame, but the thing dragged her into a cage-like embrace. Trapped, Ellen shrieked and screamed my name, her hazel eye alight with terror. Her lips quivered soundlessly.

The beast's body opened at the nexus of its legs. A wet, shining proboscis, mottled gray and green, emerged. The tip opened wide to reveal a dark mouth. Ellen struggled and begged me for help. I didn't move. The mouth covered her face and silenced her screams.

Her body bucked with spasms as her flesh cracked and dried, falling away in small, desiccated flakes. In less than a minute what had been my wife was dust that drifted to the floor.

The beast turned to me and spoke in a voice that sounded like my own. "Are you ready for the transference?"

I nodded.

The proboscis reached out and enveloped my face as it had Ellen's. A surge of vitality filled me, a radiance that flowed to every cell in my body. Ellen's soul merged with mine in a sacrament that went beyond simple earthly marriage. She fought within me but was soon overcome as my essence enveloped and absorbed her.

Now my beloved Ellen was with me forever. Along with my other wives.

The Hunger of Heaven

Mage Allia of House Themis dug her slipper-clad toe into the dry soil as she waited for the young girl. She ran a bony, liver-spotted hand over her head and looked up at the Six Houses. They towered on massive poles of blue steel above the scattered huts of the forty tribes who clawed this land for sustenance, their oblong shapes tapering to long silver points that reached to the sky.

Allia finally saw her, escorted by a servant of House Themis. She was twelve or thirteen, on the cusp of puberty, and had thick red hair parted twice, once over each ear. Her violet eyes regarded Allia with a steady maturity that belied her childish stature.

The Mage dismissed the servant. She took the girl by the arm and led her to an open elevator beneath the House. Once inside, the elevator ascended quickly, gliding past the poles.

Inside the House the members and servants of Family Themis gave way as the Mage led the girl down a bright metallic corridor to an oval door. Allia laid her hand upon the smooth surface. The door glowed with a soft luminance and swung silently inward. Allia led the girl inside and the door closed behind them.

The room was large, with smooth bluish walls that curved up to a glass ceiling, through which the pointed tip of the House could be seen as it stabbed into the hazy air above. The room was unfurnished except for a single chair of dark wood.

Quietly the girl sat in the chair and cast her face to the skylight above.

Allia stood behind her and placed her long, white fingers on either side of the girl's head. The youngster remained passive as the Mage chanted, creating vibrations deep within her throat, generating a flux of power that spread down her arms and into her fingers. The molecular structure of the Mage's fingers altered and sank into the girl's head, pushing through the skull and melting through the folds of the brain, until they came to rest upon a small gland at its base.

Allia's throat expanded, sending more energy deep into the girl's skull. The gland quivered and unlocked. A reservoir of energy flowed out, using Allia's fingers and arms as conduits and filling the Mage with power. Allia looked up through the glass ceiling to the sharp peak of the House.

The pointed tip shone with light and expanded upward like a living thing. Allia kept her focus and continued chanting as the girl quivered underneath her.

The tip of the House shot up and punched a hole in the sky. Celestial brilliance shone through. The boundaries of the hole frayed and pulled apart. Allia could hear thousands of people on the ground scream as intense, living light poured through the widening gap.

She rejoiced as the light bathed her. Every cell in her body became microscopic sponges that absorbed deistic power. She was transcendent. Nothing was visible but the voracious light as it blasted through the Mage. Allia shuddered in something close to sexual pleasure as she opened herself to omnipotence.

The power disappeared.

Allia shrieked as her hands were torn away. She fell to the floor and stared in horror as blood pumped from the stumps of her arms.

The young girl stood before her, radiating light so intense it obliterated her features.

"Who am I?" The girl demanded. Her voice lanced through Allia and House Themis and roared off into infinity.

"I don't know!" Allia screamed.

"I am who you would be," the girl said. "I am your hubris."

Mage Allia was swept up and consumed by the limitless hunger of Heaven.

Offering Day

"Oh, hey Bob! Are you here for the offering?"

Bob looked past Carl at the line that stretched to the altar. There were at least twenty people ahead of them, but this was not the Division of Motor Vehicles. This line would move quickly.

A man at the front of the line walked up two steps to an awaiting priest. The priest's headdress, made of bright blue, red, and yellow feathers, fluttered as he nodded his head, his face stern and saturnine. The man smiled and removed his shirt, then he bowed to the beautiful, multi-threaded tapestry that hung in the chancel. The tapestry bore an image of a winged, feathered serpent with shimmering coils.

The bare-chested man laid back on the thick stone of the altar. Leftover blood spattered on the stone floor. The priest raised a wide, double-edged knife and, with both hands, plunged it into the man's torso. The heavy steel sheared through ribs and opened up the chest cavity. The exposed heart, red and glistening, continued to beat as it was cut free. The priest shoved the quivering organ into the mouth of a stone effigy that resembled the head of the winged serpent on the tapestry. Thick streams of blood ran through grooves cut on either side of the altar and gurgled down a drain. The eviscerated body was dragged away by two acolytes and the next person in line ascended the stairs.

"I've been a devotee of Quetzalcoatl for years, and they finally called my name to offer to him!" Carl said, his words gushing with anticipation. "Just like you! Aren't you excited?"

Bob smiled and gave Carl a big thumbs-up. "You bet."

The line moved quickly. Within ten minutes Carl, his face rapt with joy, stepped up and in short order had his heart torn from the chest and fed to the stone effigy of the serpent god. His body was hauled away. Bob stepped up. The priest nodded at him to remove his shirt.

"Well, see, that's the thing," Bob said with discomfort. He looked away from the scowling priest. "I just got back from the doctor, and he told me I have a heart murmur. As much as I want to make my offering to the great Quetzalcoatl, I don't want to insult him by giving him a faulty heart. I'm really sorry."

The priest's glowering face softened. He clasped Bob's shoulder with a bloody hand. The feathers on his headdress danced back and forth as if in commiseration.

"I am very sorry to hear this, my son. I know how much you must have been looking forward to your offering. But you're right, the great god cannot accept your heart as it is. But perhaps with the right medical treatment your heart can be made healthy again, perhaps even in time for next year's offering."

Bob smiled gamely. "I very much hope so."

The priest patted Bob on the back, leaving red handprints on his white dress shirt. "Go in peace, my son. As devastating as this seems now, I believe this means that Quetzalcoatl has other plans for you. Rejoice in that knowledge."

Bob wiped his eyes. "You are of course right. I will try to carry on, as the great god wishes."

He stepped down and walked to the temple doors. He received nods of sympathy and words of consolation from those still in line.

Bob walked through the doors and out into the bright sunlight, his heart beating with a strong, regular rhythm.

A New Birth

The van maneuvered with care along the road. Enormous potholes threatened to swallow the vehicle's tires, and more than once the old Kikuyu driver was forced to travel on the side, over African soil the color of rust.

The tour group endured the sudden bounces and dips with stoic patience. This was, after all, part of the safari experience. They had left Nairobi and were on their way to the Treetops Hotel, an incredible structure built on stilts within the branches of a chestnut tree that overlooked watering holes that attracted elephants, rhinos, and other wildlife.

Tracy Daniels was the tour guide. Twenty-eight and a native of London, this was her tenth tour of Kenya. In the seat next to the driver, she looked out the windshield at the tall yellow grass of the savannah, dotted with acacia trees and red, castle-like termite mounds. Tracy loved Africa. She loved the people, the fauna, and the still, patient atmosphere of the continent.

This tour group was small; only a handful of people. Tracy preferred it that way. Large groups tended to be slow and disagreeable. Smaller groups got along better and saw the country at their own pace.

"I can't wait until we get to Mount Kenya Safari Club," said Connie, a plump, middle-aged woman from New York who was there with her husband Danny for their twenty-fifth wedding anniversary. "I hear that's where the movie stars stay. Maybe we'll see one!"

"I just hope we see the white rhino," said Nicole, a blonde and tanned college student from Florida. "Supposedly Treetops will be our best chance to see one. Do you think we will, Tracy?"

Tracy turned in her seat. "It's possible, but chances are it will be very late at night. They're solitary creatures and go to the watering hole when the other animals have left."

The van reached the outskirts of the town of Kiganjo. The white-haired driver, Francis, pulled over and pointed to the right. There, shockingly close, was a towering mountain of cold gray stone, dusted with drifts of ancient snow.

"Mount Kenya," Tracy said in reverence. "The second tallest mountain in Africa. Kilimanjaro is taller, but I think this mountain is more beautiful and majestic."

The tourists flocked to the van's windows and snapped pictures. Nearby, several residents from the town stood and smiled at this familiar sight.

"That is the home of Ngai, the Creator of all," said Francis. "It was he who put forth humans over the earth. The mountain is his throne, where he sits and watches us."

Tracy loved doing the Kenyan tours with Francis. A longtime driver for various tour companies, Francis was seventy, yet he proved a tireless companion, able to drive for hours over roads that made the surface of the moon look smooth. He was also friendly and helpful, and his knowledge of local mythology heightened the interest level of the tourists he shuffled all over the country.

A vibration rippled up through Tracy's feet. The van's windows rattled, and its suspension squealed as the ground shook. Outside, the town residents looked at one another in consternation.

"Is this an earthquake?" Connie grabbed her husband in panic.

"I've never heard of earthquakes in this area," Tracy was unable to keep fear out of her voice. "Francis, what—"

A sudden explosion, distant but powerful, rocked the van. The tour group screamed. The townsfolk fell to the ground and covered their heads.

The trembling stopped. All was silent. The people from the town stood and wailed in despair.

One by one the tour group looked at the mountain. A massive rift split Mount Kenya, running from its peak and zigzagging about a third of the way down. White plumes of smoke issued from the rift. A red glow emanated from its deepest recesses.

Tracy was stunned. She had heard that Mount Kenya was volcanic in origin, but she never thought she would see an eruption. Were they in any danger?

"Ngai is angered," Francis whispered. Stacy looked at him in consternation. Now was not the time for Francis to fall back on Kikuyu superstition.

"Oh my God," Connie said, her voice shaking. "Is that lava?"

Thick, red fluid spewed from the rift, countless gallons that spilled across the rocks and flooded crevices, sweeping trees and rocks in front of it like so many twigs and pebbles. The tour group heard rather than saw the deluge reach ground level, and the building crescendo left no doubt it was heading in their direction.

"It is a new birth," Francis said.

"Francis, get us out of here! Drive!" Tracy shouted.

"It is no use. We cannot run from what is to happen."

They heard the panicked screams from the townspeople.

The red liquid moved toward humans with a chilling sentience. No heat radiated from it. Though it flowed around trees, they did not burst into flame.

This is not lava, Tracy realized. *This is blood, living blood from the earth.*

Tracy watched with sick terror as the townsfolk were targeted. The blood reared up and assumed shapes that were animal and human both, red, dripping masses that had legs and claws and teeth, which tore into their victims and digested them. Once the people had been consumed, new, alien creatures stood, the blood flowing off them like crimson mercury, leaving them unmarked and naked. They were taller than humans, thinner, with larger heads and long, sinewy limbs. They looked around with eyes the color of gold.

The blood rushed toward the tour van.

Tracy screamed and tried to pull Francis from the driver's seat. He grabbed her with a strength that belied his age and brought her face close to his.

"Accept it, *binti*," he said calmly. "We cannot run from this. We have disappointed Ngai. He has chosen to replace us."

The blood reached the van. The force of the impact knocked the vehicle onto its side. Bodies fell, and twisted in desperation as the blood poured through the windows and assumed elemental shapes that ripped into the humans and fed on their flesh and bones.

\#

Zebras grazed on grass thick and green. Wildebeests and gazelles walked about serenely, even as lions and leopards stalked them. They showed no fear of the tall beings, who stood and watched.

Heir of the First

Warren squirmed in the stiff chair. The old scar on his lower right side was bothering him. His mother noticed his fidgeting and laid a thin, dry hand on his arm.

The lawyer's office was small. There were two doors, one behind Warren and one behind the lawyer's desk. Warren looked at the nameplate on the desk, where *Ephrem Advena* was embossed in gold gilt letters.

The lawyer, a short, fat little man with slicked back silver hair and glasses that reflected the overhead fluorescent light, folded his chubby hands together.

"Mr. Smoat, before his death your father and I had a long business relationship. I hope to continue that with you."

Warren had no idea what Ephrem Advena was talking about. Warren and his father hadn't spoken to each other for fifteen years. As far as Warren knew, his father had spent his last years as a professional barfly. How had he paid for Advena's services?

Warren glanced at his mother. She was small and delicate, with straight white hair framing a pale face. Her brown eyes were moist. Her smile was a simple one, a perfect enabler's smile that asked no questions. She looked twenty years older than her actual age. Warren's own dark hair and eyes matched pictures of her from a long time ago.

He looked to the lawyer. "What did you do for my father?"

"I made sure his affairs were kept in order."

A short, incredulous laugh erupted from Warren. "His affairs? What affairs? Mr. Advena, my father wasn't a man with a lot on his plate. All he cared about was where his next drink was coming from."

"You would be surprised at what your father had on his plate, Mr. Smoat."

"Like what? Look, Mr. Advena, let's be frank. My father was a drunk. What could he have possibly been doing that didn't interfere with carbonizing his liver?"

Ephrem Advena leaned forward. "Mr. Smoat, you were estranged from your father for many years. You really have no idea what he was doing. Yes, he was a drinker. Unfortunately, that seems to be a trait in your family, an ingrained response to the responsibility that is thrust upon each successor of your family line."

What the hell was this? Warren looked again at his mother, who nodded her head in affirmation of the lawyer's words.

"Excuse me, but what do you mean by saying that alcoholism is a trait passed down in my family? And what 'responsibility' are you talking about?"

The lawyer folded his hands across his girth. "Do you remember your paternal grandfather, Mr. Smoat?"

"Of course I do. It was only sixteen years ago that he died. And, yes, he was a drunk, too. So what? It doesn't mean his father was a drunk, and it certainly doesn't mean I will become one."

"I can assure you, Mr. Smoat, your grandfather's father drank excessively at the end, as his father did before him. As for you, we can only wait and see."

"Now wait a minute, how could you possibly know anything about that? I don't even know about it."

"I have been assisting your family for a long time, Mr. Smoat. I know its entire history."

Warren turned to his mother. "Mom, what do you know about this?"

"Everything Ephrem is saying is true," she said, her smile not once slipping out of place. "There is a long-standing connection between him and your family."

Your family. Not *our* family. As if she was merely the vessel chosen for his gestation.

Warren looked at Advena and shook his head. "I don't know what's going on here. Look, Mr. Advena, I don't know how my father paid for your services, but I'm pretty sure I can't afford them. I don't even know why I would need them."

Advena pushed his chair back and reached down. He lifted a wooden case, dark with age, and placed it on his desk. It was about three feet long and rectangular. He thumbed the latch and lifted the lid.

Within was a wooden walking cane that was not varnished or painted. The body of the cane was crooked, as if it had been hastily fashioned from a tree branch. Warren could see knots and grooves in the light-brown wood. The handle of the cane twisted in a curlicue design that looked natural and unforced.

The lawyer lifted the cane from the box and offered it to Warren. "This has been in your family more generations than you know," he said. "With your father's death, it now belongs to you."

Perplexed, Warren took the cane. It was lighter than he thought it would be. If it was as old as the lawyer said, then there was no way it could support anyone's weight as a walking stick.

Warren studied the curlicue design of the handle. The wood thinned as it turned on itself, creating a series of concentric circles until it came to the tip. At the tip was a tiny black triangular shape. Warren fingered it. It moved back and forth. It was a leaf. How had that stayed on for so long?

His mother's grip tightened on his arm. Her white, delicate face reflected pride, but there was something else. Warren realized it was resignation.

The empty case closed with finality. The lawyer put it back behind his desk.

"Congratulations, Warren…may I call you Warren? Please, call me Ephrem. Anyway, the cane is now yours. You will carry it until your death, and then your son will carry it."

Warren gave the cane a closer look. "What am I supposed to do with this? And how do you know I'm going to have a son? I'm not even married."

Advena chuckled. "All in good time. For now, take the cane home and get to know it." The lawyer handed Warren a business card. "When you're ready, give me a call. We'll go from there."

#

Warren's mother was silent as he drove her home. The cane lay in the back seat, an enigma she refused to talk about. In the driveway she kissed his cheek and said "farewell". Not "goodbye" or "see you later". Just "farewell". She did not look back as she unlocked the door and entered the house.

It was dusk by the time Warren returned to his apartment building. He carried the cane up the dark, narrow stairs to his apartment on the second floor. Inside, Warren put the cane down and made himself a peanut butter sandwich and chased it down with milk that was a day away from expiration. He tried to think through everything that had happened at the lawyer's office. What was so important about the cane? Why had the lawyer not once raised the issue of legal fees?

How did Advena know all about Warren's family history? And what was this "responsibility" that Warren was supposed to take on that had been his father's? That had supposedly driven his father to become a raging alcoholic?

As Warren thought about it, he realized that his father had not always been a heavy drinker. At best, he had been a moderate drinker, until…

Until shortly after his father, Warren's grandfather, had died.

And then he had pushed Warren out of his life.

Warren's mother had to know what was going on. But she responded to his questions with nothing more than a smile and silence.

For now, take the cane home and get to know it. When you're ready, give me a call.

How was he supposed to "get to know" a cane?

It was only eight in the evening, but sudden fatigue hit Warren hard. He grabbed the cane and took it into the bedroom. He set it against the nightstand next to the bed, stripped to his underwear, and went to bed.

\#

Warren sat at a small table. The table was a living thing, covered with bark. Its legs shot roots into the ground. He was outside, someplace dark and wild. Ancient trees with thick, mossy trunks watched over him.

Warren's mother sat across from him. She held the cane his father had left him.

She smiled and laid the cane on the table. "My existence is but for the fulfillment of two duties. One was giving birth to you. The other is to repower the cane".

Warren was dreaming. He knew he was dreaming. But while most dreams were fuzzy and amorphous, this one was vivid. Its clarity eclipsed that of the waking world.

But, as with all dreams, lucid or not, Warren felt compelled to act it out. "How do you repower a cane? It's not a battery."

"Yes, it is," his mother said. "A battery stores power. Once that power is used up, it needs to be recharged. The cane's power died with your father. It is now my duty to replace that power for your use."

She closed her eyes. The hairs on Warren's arms and head stood on end as static surrounded him like a swarm of hornets. His mother gasped as her form lost solidity. She became transparent.

The cane, while not changing in any perceptive way, filled with renewed energy. Warren could not say how, but he knew it was true.

His mother's body dissolved into floating wisps that settled on the cane. They melted into the wood.

Warren was scared. If he touched the cane his life would change. Warren didn't want any part of it.

His hand reached for the cane...

Warren shot out of bed. His heart raced as he took a few halting steps in the dark, unsure if he was truly awake or still in the dream. His hand found the light switch. The sudden brightness banished the dregs of his somnambulism.

The cane was where he had left it, leaning up against the nightstand. It did not look any different now than it did when he brought it home.

Fighting a sudden panic, he grabbed his cell phone and dialed his mother's number. Each unanswered ring drove a weight into his heart.

#

Very few people attended his mother's funeral. She had no family that Warren knew of, and almost no one from his father's side had bothered to come.

Warren looked at the lonely casket, sitting on the frame above the cement-lined hole where it would be lowered. It had been placed there by professional pallbearers from the funeral home. A single red rose rested on top, placed there by Warren.

"This is a difficult time, I know," said a voice behind him. "But we need to talk."

Warren turned and faced Ephrem Advena.

"Look, Mr. Advena, this isn't a good time," Warren said. "My father's cane is not high on my list of priorities right now."

"It's not your father's cane, it's your cane," Advena said. "And as such, it needs to be at the top of your priority list. Your mother knew its importance. That's why she gave her life for it."

Ice gripped Warren's heart. "What do you mean she gave her life for it?"

"Come now, Warren. You watched her transfer her power, her life, into the cane. It seemed to be a dream, but of course it wasn't. It happened in a reality other than this. One of many you will deal with, now that the cane is yours."

Warren could not speak. The air seemed to thicken around him.

"Go home, Warren. Take up the cane. Get to know it. Then come to my office and see me. I'm available at any time."

The round man walked away.

\#

Warren stared at the cane. It looked so *ordinary*. Granted, the curlicue design of the handle, with that strange little leaf at the end, made it stand out a bit, but still.

Why was he so afraid to touch it?

True, the dream he had on the night his mother died, plus Advena's inexplicable affirmation of the dream, disturbed him. The lawyer himself disturbed him. What was Advena's interest in Warren and the cane? Nothing made sense.

He had to do something. He couldn't leave the cane leaning against the night stand, to stare at every morning when he woke up. At the very least it had to go into the closet.

Shaking off his hesitation, Warren grabbed the curlicue handle.

His hand disappeared, melting into the swirling design. Warren felt no pain or any other physical sensation as the cane became an extension of his right arm.

Incomprehension gave way to horror. Warren's throat squeezed shut and he shook his arm, trying to dislodge the cane and retrieve his hand.

Energy within the cane, energy his mother's life created, traveled up his arm and permeated his body. It flowed to his brain, seeping into every crevice, taking over every synapse and transformed it into a new creation, a tool with one set purpose.

Numerous realities flashed around Warren in a rapid-fire sequence. Worlds that defied ordinary human perception opened to him. He saw sentient beings of light, elemental creatures of energy, human thoughts made solid and given room to roam, places where color was an invasive species and vibrations ruled over all. These existences slid by like pages being flipped in an endless book. And they all filled Warren's mind, his very being, to the point where he felt he would burst, his every molecule blowing up and subdividing to shed the enormity of all...

"Stop!"

The differing realities slowed down, and then stopped at one.

It was a place of desolation and pollution. The remains of what may have been buildings were scattered across a smoking landscape. Creatures prowled close to the blackened ground, scuttling along on multiple limbs. They had faces within their torsos, human faces, with wide, hungry eyes and mouths filled with razor teeth. The stronger creatures ambushed the weaker ones, who screamed with very human voices as they were eaten.

It did not take long for them to notice Warren standing in their midst.

A group of five approached. They *smiled* as they stalked him. Like spiders, the creatures jumped, their claws poised to tear into Warren

Warren forced the words through his panic. "Get me out of here!"

The cane powered and the scene shifted.

He was now in a place that seemed constructed of glass. Tiny crystal globes floated through the air. A few bounced off his body like sleet.

Something swirled in the distance. It moved in a circular motion, like a tornado, but it wasn't anywhere near as big. It skimmed over the flat, glassine ground and sent crystal globes scattering. It headed straight at Warren.

It broke apart, sending out slivers of wind that darted between the crystals. The slivers did not fly about mindlessly; they had direction, and purpose. They congregated into a swarm, flew forward, and surrounded Warren.

The snippets of wind zipped by his face like angry wasps. A few brushed his skin. The contact stung. Warren brought his left hand to his face. It came away bloody.

A few landed on the back of his neck. Thin needles pricked his skin and pushed deeper, looking for his spinal column.

Warren screamed and ran, trying with his left hand to dislodge the things on his neck. Crystals bounced off his face.

"Get me home!"

Warren fell to his knees onto something that was not glass. He scratched at his eyes and neck, but nothing was there. Warren realized that his right hand was now free.

He looked around his bedroom. The cane was lying on the floor in front of him.

He pushed himself up on unsteady legs. Warren could not stop looking around. He waited for the scene to shift, his bedroom replaced by some horrible alternate world.

Everything remained as it was. Apparently, for now, the ride was over.

Warren's face stung from where the wind wasps had touched him. He went to the bathroom and looked in the mirror.

Though he had stopped bleeding, his face was peppered with tiny slices that looked like paper cuts. He touched the back of his neck. It was sore.

He hadn't imagined anything. It was all real.

Warren took off his shirt and looked at the small scar on his right side, near the bottom of his ribcage. He had no idea how he had gotten it; it had been with him for as long as he could remember. He had asked his parents about it, but they never given him more than a vague, hurried answer, something about an accident when Warren was an infant. But it didn't look like a scar from an accident. It was straight and smooth, as if made by a surgeon's scalpel.

It had never bothered him until the day he had stepped into Ephrem Advena's office. Now he found himself conscious of it in a way he had never been. Warren shook his head and left the bathroom.

In the bedroom, he stood and stared at the cane.

\#

Ephrem Advena was not surprised at Warren's unannounced visit, or at the condition of Warren's face.

"I see you took up the cane."

Warren stood in front of the lawyer's desk. He had to restrain himself from punching the fat man in the face.

"What the fuck is that thing? What did it do to me?"

"I suppose I should have warned you about your first use. When it has a fresh charge, the cane can be quite active. Excitable, if such an emotion can be attributed to it. But if I had tried to warn you, you wouldn't have believed me. You needed to see for yourself."

"See for myself? That thing became a part of me. Then it brought me to places where things tried to kill me. Look at my face! It was only through luck that I escaped."

Advena shook his head. "No, it wasn't luck. You told the cane what you wanted, and it obeyed. That is its purpose. You are its bearer. You control it."

"How the hell do I control it? The cane brought me to places I didn't want to go. How do I stop that?"

"The cane only did what it is intended to do. Think of it as a key that unlocks doors that are not otherwise accessible. What lies beyond those doors are your responsibilities. As they were your father's, and his father's, and so on."

Warren stared at him. "What could I possibly be responsible for in these places? I don't know what they are. I don't know what rules they play by. They're fucking dangerous!"

"Yes, they are dangerous. That is because they have lost balance. It is your job to restore that balance."

"How am I supposed to do that? What can I do that my father and ancestors could not?"

"Your father and ancestors did fine," Advena said. "They brought balance to myriad realities. You're missing the fact that there are countless worlds. Existence is infinite. There will always be worlds that lose their balance and need to be brought back in line. This is a continuous job. You do what you can, and then when you're gone, your son takes over, and then his son, and then his son... do you understand now?"

Warren paced the office as much as the room's small dimensions allowed. "What if I don't have a son? Who's to say I'll get married, or whether we'll have any kids, or if I have daughters instead of sons?"

Advena smiled and stood up from his chair. He walked to the closed door behind his desk. "That's all taken care of."

He opened the door. A beautiful woman about Warren's age stood on the other side. She had long dark hair and deep brown eyes. She looked at Warren and smiled as if she had known him for years.

"Warren, meet your wife, Rebecca."

Rebecca walked around the desk and took Warren's hand. His head spun as he tried to fathom what was going on.

"My wife? I don't know this woman. Who is she?"

"I already told you, Warren. Her name is Rebecca. She is your wife."

The lawyer picked up a folder, opened it, and took out a piece of paper. "Here is your marriage license. Rebecca has already signed it. The witness is of course me. All it needs is your signature." Advena took a gold-plated pen from his shirt pocket and passed it along with the paper to Warren.

Rebecca kissed his cheek. "Hurry up and sign it, so we can go home and…" She turned his head and gave him a meaningful kiss on the lips. "Get to work conceiving our son."

Despite the situation, Warren grew aroused. But it was too weird. He separated himself from the dark-haired woman.

"I don't know what's going on, but this isn't right." He groped for the door knob behind him. "I don't care what my father was, or anyone else before him. I'm getting rid of that cane. I'm no 'bearer', as you call it. I want nothing to do with any of this."

Advena shook his head as if he had expected this response. Rebecca gave him a look of amused tolerance which said *my husband is having another one of his moods. He'll get over it.*

"Okay, Warren, play it your way. All it does is delay the inevitable. Trust me, once you accept who you are, the sooner you will make peace with it and get on with what you have to do."

"Make peace with it? By becoming an alcoholic like my father? Is that how I make peace with it?"

"That doesn't need to happen, Warren. I believe you are stronger than your father. And you will have Rebecca by your side."

Warren gave Rebecca a long look. "Where does she come from, anyway?"

"She was brought into being and raised in a controlled environment," Advena said. "Her purpose is to assist and support you. She has been genetically modified to bear only one child. A son."

Rebecca's smile widened in a display of love.

"Just like your mother and grandmother before her, and all of your great-grandmothers before that."

Warren found the knob and pulled the door open. "No," he muttered as he backed out of the office. He turned and fled.

"See you tomorrow, Warren!" Ephrem Advena called out.

#

She was so beautiful, and perfect for him. They were made for each other. Literally. So why was he resisting?

Rebecca stood by his bed and shed her clothes. His body ached with desire. Warren's clothes melted off him. It was the most natural thing in the world. His penis was so stiff it hurt. His hands found Rebecca's marvelously smooth shoulders and he bent forward to kiss her...

Rebecca pushed him away gently, her smile full of things to come. "First things first," she said. She gave him a piece of paper and a pen. As quickly as he could Warren scribbled his name on the line. The paper and pen disappeared from his hands.

Rebecca wrapped her arms around his neck. "Now we can consummate our marriage," she said as she drew him to the bed...

Warren woke as his penis became flaccid. A soft hand touched his arm.

"Good morning, husband," Rebecca said. "I hope you saved something for round two."

#

Warren sat in Ephrem Advena's office. He had no fight left in him. Rebecca stood by his side, her hand resting comfortably on his shoulder.

Advena looked at him with something that resembled sympathy. "I'm glad you've come to accept this, Warren. Believe me when I say this is going to open up your life. You may even enjoy it. Not all of your ancestors did this unwillingly. Many actually thrived once they embraced it."

Warren looked up. "What am I? What is it about my family line that makes us different from everybody else?"

The lawyer sat back. "That's a question that can be answered in many ways. The most succinct answer I can give is to say that your oldest ancestor was the First."

"The first what?"

"The First, Warren," Advena said, enunciating the capitalization. "The First Man. The first human to arrive and populate this planet."

Warren tried to rein in his confusion. "What do you mean, the First Man? Like the first Neanderthal or something?"

"No, Warren. I mean like Adam."

Warren could not speak. He looked up at Rebecca, who smiled and nodded.

"Hundreds of thousands of years ago," Advena said. "Your ancestor came to this planet, which was on the cusp of great change. The predominant life form that had ruled for millions of years was long extinct. It was a time of uncertainty and chaos. There was a real threat of all species facing extinction. In short, this world was out of balance. This is what your ancestor was sent here to fix."

Warren lowered his head into his hands. He didn't want to listen to any more.

Ephrem Advena came from around the desk and stood in front of Warren. "Hearing it from me won't make you believe or understand it. You need to *see* it. Go home, Warren. Go home and take up the cane. It will show you what you need to know."

#

Warren sat on his bed and stared at the cane. Rebecca was next to him. She ran her fingers through his hair.

He looked at her. For the first time he noticed certain similarities between her features and his. If he had a sister, she would look like Rebecca. Come to think of it, his mother and father had looked remarkably alike. The pain in his side flared.

50

Rebecca gazed back, giving herself to him, her presence providing stability and support. Warren felt a closeness to her that belied the short time they had known each other.

He reached out and took the cane.

Once more the wooden curlicue handle enveloped his hand. Reality shifted around Warren; his bedroom and Rebecca drifted off.

"Show me my lineage," he told the cane.

Warren looked down on a green world. The earth was in a transition period between dominant animal species; right now plants ruled over all. Flowers the size of buses bloomed, their reds and yellows and violets caught sunlight and drank it in. Bees the size of kittens dipped into each flower, gathering pollen and moving on. Trees rose hundreds of feet into the air, the diameter of their trunks fifty feet across. Roots, twisting like gigantic snakes, sought the warm earth. Ferns with leaves that curled and bent as if sentient carpeted the rich, nutritious soil.

Mammals dotted the landscape. Most were small, no bigger than dogs. A few were the size of rhinos. Reptiles stayed well hidden, and the birds had toothy beaks, with feathers that resembled scales.

Yet Warren sensed a dissonance. The animals were not breeding as they should, and their offspring were often born dead. Disease eradicated the bees and other pollinators; he now saw the plants, though huge, were dying. They were too many, with not enough nutrients to go around. The same was true of the oceans. Plankton and small fish were not replicating like they should. The entire food chain was in danger of collapsing.

The planet was less than a thousand years from becoming an empty, barren rock.

A light beamed down from the sky, an alien illumination whose source Warren could not see. It lit an open patch of ground. A figure materialized within it, one that was unmistakably human.

It was a man, with features that bore a strong resemblance to Warren's own.

The light disappeared. The man was nude. He stood in place, surrounded by a protective, iridescent barrier that shimmered blues, greens, and reds as the sun moved across the sky. A small, sudden wound appeared on the man's side. Genetic material was removed from a rib by an unseen collector, and the wound was patched over and healed.

Time sped up. Days flipped past in rapid succession. The man, never showing any signs of fatigue or awareness of his surroundings, continued to stand in one spot. Next to him the material taken from his body expanded and grew, sealed within a separate protective space. Cells formed and split and created more cells. Warren recognized the shape of a fetus, which zipped through gestation in a matter of hours. It was female.

The fetus became an infant, which grew into adolescence and finally into adulthood. The woman and man opened their eyes simultaneously. The protective shields around them disappeared.

Another beam of light came from the sky. It was thinner than the one that had brought the man. It hit the open ground and pushed through the soil. The light winked out.

Seconds later a plant broke through the soil. The sapling twisted up and sprouted branches tipped with dark, triangular leaves. The trunk was smooth and round.

The new tree was not as tall as those surrounding it, but its presence made the others shrink in significance. Everything seemed to bend to the new growth.

The man approached the tree and reached for a low, thin branch. The tip of the branch wrapped around his hand. The man spoke words that Warren could not hear. He pulled his hand away. The branch came with him. The man's right hand was a curlicue handle with a small leaf at the tip. Three feet of wood made up the rest.

The man spoke to the cane. His figure shimmered and expanded, losing definition as it shot particles in every direction. Traveling at a speed that Warren couldn't follow, each particle broke down into even finer particles which immersed themselves into everything: plants, animals, the very earth itself.

Change happened that Warren could not describe in physical terms. Something huge, something essential, *shifted*. It occurred everywhere. Warren felt a sudden lurch within his own psyche.

The man reformed, the cane still attached to his hand. With one word it detached itself.

The man turned to the woman. He took her to the ground and copulated with her.

More days flew by. Weeks, then months, passed by in less than a minute as the man and woman settled upon the land, building a shelter made of stone and tilling the soil to grow crops for food and clothing.

The woman gave birth to twins. Both were boys. The oldest had genetic material taken from his rib, as his father had. The resulting female, while protected, was allowed to gestate and grow in a natural time sequence. She was modified to produce only one child, a son.

Twenty years passed, the time going by within minutes to Warren's perception. On the same day that the oldest twin claimed his wife, the youngest knelt on the ground and offered up his life. His brother took it, and the body was broken down to its base molecules. These were fused with those of newly created, intelligent bipedal creatures. These hybrid beings multiplied and migrated throughout the world, taking with them the story of their creation.

It was decided that this world would make a good home.

Generations passed. Each cane bearer was succeeded by his only child, always a son. The list stopped at Warren.

"Home," Warren said.

The cane rested against the night stand. Rebecca's grip tightened on his arm.

He looked at her. His female self, created from his rib.

#

"So, Warren," Ephrem Advena said. "Do you finally understand?"

"Who are you?" Warren asked. "You say you've been assisting my family for all this time. How?"

Advena stood from his chair. His skin and clothes fell away. What stood in his place was tall and slim, with shimmering, iridescent skin and silver eyes.

"I have no actual name," the creature said. "But my primary purpose is that of guardianship. Granted, I don't have a flaming sword, but I think I've done a pretty good job so far."

#

It was a non-stop job. Once Warren got the hang of it, especially when it came to balancing out a world while in a disembodied state, it came quite naturally to him. But the number of asymmetric worlds was infinite. The sheer enormity of the task wore on him. After each use of the cane Warren found himself craving a drink.

#

Rebecca's due date arrived. She was not at the hospital; she had insisted on giving birth at home, with only Warren there to help. Warren was not thrilled at this choice; at the very least, he had wanted Advena there. Rebecca had flatly refused.

He had the hot water and the towels and everything else he thought he'd need. Of course his experience in baby delivering was zero. Although her face contorted with each contraction, Rebecca gave Warren much needed moral support.

"You can do this, Warren! The head should be crowning soon. Right about...argh!"

With a small gout of fluid, the head appeared. Warren reached out with clean hands to support it as it slid out. Rebecca screamed once more and the shoulders popped free. Once that happened the rest of the baby came out easily, quickly followed by the placenta.

Warren wrapped the baby in a towel and used a pair of sterilized scissors to cut the umbilical cord. The infant had a thatch of thick, dark hair. It opened up its eyes and regarded its father with unsettling awareness.

Rebecca cried with joy and sat up. Warren brought the bundle to her. She took the baby out of the towel.

It was a girl.

Something shifted deep within Warren, a psychic resettlement of known reality. He gasped and looked at Rebecca. She smiled.

Warren looked at her without comprehension. "How did you know?"

"It was time," Rebecca said. She wiped a sweaty lock of hair from her forehead and gazed lovingly at the girl, who began to squall. "This world is out of balance. It's too male-centric. But it's an imbalance you can't do anything about. As a male, you are blind to it. But the wives have always known it."

Rebecca kissed her daughter's forehead. "The tipping point has been reached. Existence has spoken. After you, my dear Warren, a female will be the bearer of the cane."

She was right. Now that it was spoken out, Warren sensed it. This world was suffering a significant imbalance. He wondered how Ephrem Advena would take to the news.

"What should we name her?" Warren asked.

"Eve?" Rebecca said teasingly.

"Let's not hang that on her," Warren said.

"Of course not," Rebecca agreed. "How about Dawn?"

Warren caressed the baby girl's cheek.

"Yes. Dawn."

<u>Dearest One</u>

The stack of envelopes, once three hundred and sixty-six thick, was down to two.

Danny looked out the floor to ceiling windows of his twentieth-floor apartment. Central Park always looked its best in the early morning light. He brushed back a lock of gray hair and turned to the two envelopes. His hand shook as he picked up the nearest one. He held it for a long time before he summoned the will to open it.

Like all the others, the envelope contained a single sheet of cream-colored paper. The letter was written in longhand, with a feminine, graceful flow. The salutation was always the same.

Dearest one.

Danny closed his eyes. He didn't want to read the rest. But he had to. It was part of the agreement.

You have been brought a long way. You have had three hundred and sixty-four desires sated. Nothing has been denied you. You have lived a year others can only fantasize about. Each letter has brought you a new day of joy. This letter will be no different. Your ultimate desire has been saved for last. Enjoy.

A soft knock echoed from the apartment door. Danny took a deep breath, his mind whirling with emotions too numerous to distinguish. *It's her.* He walked on numb feet. He grasped the knob, and after a second's hesitation opened the door.

She was tall and thin, with straight blonde hair that ran down her shoulders. Her blue eyes shone with a love of life that Danny knew well. She was every bit as young and beautiful as he remembered. She hadn't aged in twenty years. But then, she wouldn't. The dead don't age.

"Susan," Danny said. He did not move.

The young woman smiled. "May I come in, Danny?"

Danny quickly stepped to the side. "Yes, please, come in."

Susan walked into the five million dollar apartment. She was wearing a pantsuit, the same she had been wearing on the day the brakes had failed on her car. "Nice place."

"Thank you." Danny watched Susan explore every room.

When she was through she stood before him. "Was it worth it, Danny? Was everything worth it?"

Danny paused. "Everything before today? No. But Lilitu knew what I really wanted. You were saved for the last day. And now that you're here," Danny swallowed. "Yes, it's worth it."

Susan ran her smooth fingers through Danny's hair. She pulled him forward and kissed him. When they parted Danny was shaking and crying.

"Susan, I've missed you so much. I love you."

Susan smiled. "I love you too, Danny. Today is important for the both of us. We have to make every second count."

Danny took Susan's hand. They looked at each other in silent understanding and walked to the bedroom.

#

Morning broke with a cold and lifeless light. Danny lay in bed for as long as he dared. He had not felt Susan leave, even though he had lain awake all night.

In the place she had lain on the bed was the final envelope.

With a surprisingly steady hand Danny picked it up. He opened the flap and took out the lone sheet of cream-colored paper.

Dearest one.

It is time.

The room darkened. Danny's shivered as Lilitu's cold essence embraced his soul. The physical world fell away. Danny uttered two final words.

"Thank you."

Waiting for You

"I'm waiting for you."

The corpse's eyes were the color of spoiled milk. Desiccated lips pulled back over teeth sitting loosely in gums as black as ink. The dried, brittle body was held together by thick, agglutinant strands, the same material used to write the message on the ground a few feet away.

Sheriff Bonn's boot brushed against a finger. It snapped off. Particles of flesh wafted in the breeze. The forensic team leader, trying to preserve the scene, cast Bonn a dark look which he ignored.

He turned to his deputy. "Is that who I think it is?"

Eric Essel tipped back his hat and wiped sweat from his brow. "It sure looks like Jody Corman to me."

The shriveled body had, just a day earlier, been one of the biggest men in the county. Yet here he was, without a single drop of moisture anywhere within his gray, papery skin.

Jody Corman's shirt was open. Two puncture wounds gaped in the center of his chest. The skin around the holes was blackened, as if exposed to a caustic material.

"The spider," said Deputy Essel.

Sheriff Bonn nodded. "Yep."

"We have to talk to her."

A car pulled up containing the county medical examiner. The tall man nodded at Bonn and Essel and looked at the remains. "Another one. That makes five so far." He turned away and instructed his assistant to prepare for body removal.

Bonn looked at Essel. "What makes you think she'll agree to help us now?"

"Common human decency?"

Bonn snorted. "Yeah, right. Let's go."

#

Mary Muffet brushed back a tuft of brown hair and opened the door. Her hands were red and chafed from lye soap. She did not smile at the two visitors.

Sheriff Bonn cleared his throat. "Miss Muffet? Could we have a word?"

Mary Muffet didn't blink. "I'm very busy right now, Sheriff."

"Another body has been found," Deputy Essel said. "Jody Corman. I believe you knew him."

Mary felt a moment of recognition and pain. Her countenance reasserted itself.

"Of course I knew Jody. Everyone knew Jody."

"But you dated him for a time, isn't that right?"

Mary glared at the deputy. "That was a long time ago. I haven't talked to Jody in months."

"Look," the sheriff said, raising his hands in supplication. "It's not our intention to get into your personal life. The fact remains that Jody Corman is dead, and that he was killed by the same creature responsible for four other deaths in this town over the past year. The same message was found by Jody's body as the others."

Mary shook her head. "What does this have to do with me?"

"You're the first one the spider ever appeared to," Bonn said. "And the only one who survived the encounter."

"Why did the spider let you live?" Essel asked. "What happened on that day?"

"I've already told you, many times, what happened. I took a walk in the forest. I sat at the base of a tree, and then I noticed movement from above. It was a spider, as big as a man. So, I ran."

"Did the spider give chase?" asked Bonn.

"I don't know. I was too busy running."

"What did the spider look like?"

Mary sighed. "I've already told you this. It was covered in brown hair. It had eight enormous legs tipped with claws. It had six or eight eyes, black, the size of eggs. It had long fangs that dripped venom. Basically, it was like any other spider, only much bigger."

"You saw all that in the brief time you looked up into the tree?" asked the deputy.

Mary gripped the door and inched it closed. "Look, this has all been covered already. I have nothing more to tell you. Hopefully you'll find the spider and kill it soon. In the meantime, I'm very busy helping my mother. She's elderly and can't do a lot for herself anymore. So if you'll excuse me..."

"The spider is intelligent," Sheriff Bonn said before the door clicked shut. "It knows how to write. It may even know how to speak. Did the spider say anything to you, Miss Muffet?"

The door froze in place. Mary looked out, shook her head, and closed the door.

\#

Mary's mother rocked gently in her chair. Her white hair fell in a brittle cascade down her back. Her eyes had a thin layer of film, but there was nothing wrong with her hearing.

"He's not going to give up," she said as Mary walked into the room.

"We've been through this already," Mary said. *Jody Corman is dead.* "It's not going to happen."

"Then he'll keep killing the unispecies. They don't matter to him. All that matters is you."

It didn't have to happen. "No!" Mary turned her back on her mother. She grabbed the dust cloth and turned her attention to the old, walnut clock in the corner of the room. She rubbed the wood furiously. For several minutes the only sounds were the hum of the clock's inner workings and the crisp click of the pendulum as it reached the top of each arc.

"Maybe one of the unispecies will kill him," Mary said softly.

The old woman snorted. "You know better than that. No member of the unispecies is a match for a *na'ashjeii.*"

"I can't be the last one," Mary said in a voice full of sorrow.

"I'm sorry, my dear. You are. As is he."

Mary dropped the dust cloth and sat next to her mother. She grabbed the old woman's cold hand and held it as she cried.

"Then I have to go, if for no other reason than to stop the killing."

The mother turned to the daughter. Underneath the translucent film her eyes were as black as pitch.

"If the unispecies mean something to you, then yes."

\#

Mary's bare feet crunched on leaves and dead twigs as she walked between the trees. She held her robe closed around her neck. Little sunlight penetrated the forest canopy; even during the brightest part of the day the air was thick with shadows. But Mary's eyes were keen, and she needed little illumination to show her the way.

She stopped after two hours of walking. She was deep enough. She found a spot at the base of an ancient elm and sat down.

She did not have long to wait.

Mary heard the rustle of the leaves above as something large moved through the branches. She didn't look up. He would come down to her.

He fell with a grace that belied his size. His eight legs hit the ground at the same time, hardly disturbing the forest detritus underneath. His abdomen, covered with coarse brown hair, settled to the ground. His forelegs straightened, pushing up his thorax and head. Thick hair surrounded six-inch fangs. Obsidian eyes, two large ones and four smaller ones, reflected multiple images of Mary's face within their depths.

She rose from the leaf-strewn ground.

"Mary," the spider said, the words coming out in a choked, sibilant parody of human speech. "I see my messages got through. In which form would you prefer me?"

Mary's face was emotionless. "It doesn't matter."

"Very well. I shall join you in your form."

Four of the spider's limbs cracked and shrunk back within the body. The abdomen deflated, shrinking until it disappeared between the hind legs, which grew human feet and toes. The fangs drew back into a human head, and the six eyes morphed into two. The man that stood before Mary was tall and naked, with long brown hair flowing down his back and dark eyes that were sharp and focused.

"Does this meet to your satisfaction, my dear?"

Mary stood. "I am not your 'dear'. I do not want to do this."

"But you must. We are the last."

"So I'm told." Mary pulled open the robe and let it drop to her feet. Her nude body felt cool from the breeze that pushed stealthily through the trees.

The man smiled and stepped forward. He took Mary in his arms. "Don't you want to know my name?"

Mary did not return the embrace. "No. I have no use for it."

"Very well."

The man pulled Mary to the ground. She did not resist. Upon the robe she had brought, they copulated.

The man's shrinking penis slid out of Mary and he stood. "There. That wasn't so bad, was it?"

Mary felt the male seed traveling within her. It would suffice.

She stood. Thick nubs protruded from her body, two to a side. They grew out and elongated, as did her arms and legs. Dense brown hair sprouted from the new limbs. Hands and feet turned into gripping claws. Mary's abdomen blew out behind her legs like a balloon, becoming full and bloated. Her face reconfigured itself, the two eyes splitting into six and the mouth twisting into a dark cavern that pushed out two black, foot-long fangs. When the transformation was complete the spider that was Mary was twice the size of the spider from which the man had changed.

Her mate smiled and bowed his head. He did not transform back into a spider, nor did he try to run.

Mary's forelimb shot forward and snagged the man by the neck. She pulled him to her and bit his head off. Her fangs sank into his quivering torso and pumped in toxin. His organs, muscles, and bones liquefied within seconds. Mary feasted until the body was a dry and empty shell.

\#

Mary dialed the sheriff's number.

"Sheriff Bonn? This is Mary Muffet. Look, I'm sorry about the way I treated you earlier. I know where the spider is… no, actually, it's dead… I think you need to bring Deputy Essel with you… yes, I'll explain it all when you get here."

She hung up. Her mother smiled and rocked in her chair.

\#

Mary sat with her mother and looked at the sack that hung from the ceiling. At first glance it appeared to be a large sack of potatoes. But there were thousands of pearly white spheres inside.

A tight-knit, thick web strung out from the bottom of the sack to the floor. Within, two objects were bound tight.

"I know you didn't want to do this," her mother said. "But I'm glad you did."

Mary held her mother's hand. "I guess I just wanted to live in peace with the unispecies. I felt as long as I looked like them, they would accept me, and everything would be fine. I tried so hard to be like them. But I am not one of them."

"No, you are not. You are a *na'ashjeii*, the last egg-bearing female. Your mate was the last seed-bearing male."

Mary looked at the sack. "At least for now."

The sack jerked to the side and swung by the adhesive that held it to the ceiling. Tens, then hundreds, of hatching babies squirmed within. The stronger ones turned on their weaker siblings and consumed them. The eggs continued to hatch. The tight, violent struggle continued. The sack burst open and the surviving young spread out on the webbing. They clustered there, pale and thick. Only a few would live to adulthood, an equal amount of females and males.

It would be enough.

They gathered around the meal their mother left for them.

From within their sticky prisons Sheriff Bonn and Deputy Essel screamed as thousands of newborns started to feed.

Mary felt a twinge of guilt. "I should have used a deer. They're going to suffer."

"No," her mother said. "They were too inquisitive. They would have pieced together what happened, then you and I would have been hunted down and killed, and all of these young would have been burned."

Mary knew her mother was right. She had tried too long to assimilate with the unispecies, who had infested and taken over a world they should have shared and drove the *na'ashjeii* to the verge of extinction.

The guilt fluttered and died.

Jean and Charlie: A Ghost Story of Love and Infidelity

The window was weather-stained and streaked with grit. Jean peered through the few spots that provided a view of the overgrown front yard. To the left of the yellow grass a broken driveway twisted toward the house. The asphalt was riddled with faults, many of them sprouting thick clumps of weeds. With the continuous freezing and thawing of each passing winter the cracks grew wider, sending oily chunks of macadam to the surface to ambush a car's tires. But the last car that used this driveway had long ago moved on. It had been many years since Charlie's teal green Chevy Bel Air, with its sleek fins and cats-eye taillights, pulled out of this driveway and roared off into the night, its V8 engine growling like a predator on the hunt.

Jean looked at her reflection in the brittle glass. It amazed her she could still cast a reflection, though the image was vague and lost definition with each passing year. Her dark hair, done up in a "shag" hairdo, was still the same, every bit as fresh as the day she had gotten it done at Paulette's Hair Salon forty years ago.

The same day Charlie decided to end their 10-year marriage.

Jean had suspected there was another woman. There were nights when Charlie came home reeking of whiskey. Charlie would apologize, saying he had lost track of time because he was out with the guys. But underneath the revolting stench of alcohol there was another scent, one that could not be disguised with booze: the odor of another woman.

The late nights grew more frequent. Jean knew she had to confront her husband. She summoned her courage, and on the last night of their marriage she did.

Charlie staggered in, drunk as always. His black hair was disheveled and poked like unkempt shrubbery around his oversized ears. His bushy eyebrows rose in shock when Jean told him she knew he was running around with another woman.

Charlie was not a big man, but he was bigger than Jean and when his fist shot out it had enough power to shatter her nose and send her crashing to the hardwood floor. Blood gushed down Jean's throat. She couldn't breathe. Charlie straddled her and grabbed twin handfuls of hair. He yanked her bloodied face up toward his and slammed her head down on the unyielding wood. Bright lights exploded behind Jean's eyes. Charlie lifted her face back up and sent her head crashing down again, and again. The sound of Jean's head hitting the floor changed from sharp cracks to liquid splatters.

Jean sighed and turned from the window. After Charlie sobered up to what he had done, he had dragged her limp body down the musty wooden stairs into the basement and stashed her corpse in a hidden alcove behind a faux-pine paneled wall. He then cleaned up the blood and took off in the Bel Air. He had not returned in the forty years since, while Jean's ghost walked the house and her bones moldered in the basement.

Still, Jean kept a watch for Charlie. He would return. He had no choice, for this was the town of Bertram's Cross. It is said of Las Vegas that what happens there stays there. The same could be said for Bertram's Cross. The town trapped the spirits of all its inhabitants, no matter how far away their physical bodies traveled. In the end, they all returned.

Even though Charlie had been in his late twenties on the night he had driven away, he lived life hard. He loved his drink. That, Jean was sure, had never changed. After forty years the toxic excess would have ravaged his body.

It wouldn't be long now.

As dusk fell over Bertram's Cross a pair of headlights from a long, old Chevy appeared at the end of the empty street. Jean smiled.

Welcome home, Charlie.

The wide tires of the Bel Air made no sound as the car pulled into the debris-strewn driveway. The automobile was no more physical than its occupant; the actual vehicle had long since been reduced to scrap metal. Yet to Jean it still looked the same; the teal green paint looked as fresh as the day Charlie had proudly driven it home.

Charlie, however, was another story.

Jean almost didn't recognize the form that opened the driver's door and stumbled out. The movements were jerky and showed a marked lack of willingness. Charlie's hair, what was left of it, was now completely white. The wrinkles on his face were more like fissures. His eyes were red and watery, an indication of the chronic alcoholism that had finally done him in. Jean marveled that Charlie had lasted this long. For someone who had died in his late sixties, Charlie looked twenty years older.

Charlie's herky-jerky motions continued as he walked up the front steps. He did not want to come inside the house. His rheumy eyes were bright with panic.

Too bad, Charlie. The front door's unlocked, just as you left it. Get your worthless ass in here.

Jean felt the house tremble with an anticipation that mirrored her own. After so long, the house had become an extension of her will.

Charlie stopped at the door. Jean had waited forty years for this. She adjusted her composition to push her arm through the solid wood of the door and grabbed the ragged shirt her erstwhile husband had died in. She pulled him through. Jean nearly laughed as she saw Charlie's shocked face come through the door and into the house. Once he was all the way through the door Jean pushed him down and gave his ghost just enough corporeal form to feel the pain as he tumbled to the hardwood floor of the living room.

"Hello, Charlie," Jean said, as sweet as could be. "It's been awhile. How's every little thing?"

Charlie sat on the floor, his mouth open in fear. He scuttled back and bumped against the wall that separated the living room from the dining room. "What's going on? What am I doing here?"

"Why, you're dead, Charlie. Don't you remember dying? Or were you, as usual, too drunk to know what was going on?"

Charlie's head shook back and forth. "I ain't dead. I went to sleep, and I dreamed I was in my old Bel Air, which drove me here. I didn't wanna come, but I couldn't stop it. I ain't dead. This is just a nightmare."

Jean chuckled. "How typical of you to believe that. How is it you lasted as long as you did? Your liver must have been hard enough to crack diamonds."

Charlie slowly stood, though he made sure there was plenty of distance between himself and Jean. "You're exactly as I remember. You haven't gotten any older."

"Ghosts don't age, Charlie. You have to be physical to age. Thanks to you, I haven't been physical for forty years."

Renewed fear shone in Charlie's eyes. "I didn't mean for that to happen, Jean. That was an accident. You have to believe me! I didn't mean it!"

"Sure, Charlie, I believe you. You *accidentally* slammed my head into the floor until it was mush, then you *accidentally*

71

dragged my body down into the basement and *accidentally* hid it behind a wall, then you *accidentally* cleaned up the mess and *accidentally* ran off for the next three decades. How could I have mistaken it for anything else?"

"I was drunk and scared! I didn't want to hurt you. I loved you!"

Jean's ghost solidified and glided closer to Charlie. "You *dare* say that you loved me? Is that why you screwed around with Betsy St. Clair?"

Charlie eyes widened in shock, and his arms opened in a bid to plead his case.

Jean's words came out in a sharp gust. "Your return here is not going to go well for you, Charlie. If you deny your infidelity I will make it much, much worse."

Resignation creased Charlie's face. "How did you find out who it was?"

"It really wasn't that hard. Not once I figured out what to do. You called her on our telephone to set up your drunken trysts when I was out shopping or at the hairdresser. That kept her identity from me while I was alive. But when I was dead I did some experimenting. I had plenty of time to experiment. I found out that telephone lines and electrical wires are great conduits for ghosts. I can travel all over Bertram's Cross through those lines. It's quite the thing, Charlie. Too bad you'll never get the chance to experience it."

Jean hadn't thought it was possible for a ghost to turn pale, but Charlie was proving her wrong.

"I also discovered that there is a residual memory in the phone from all the numbers that have been dialed from it. I recognized all of them except for one. Guess whose? Imagine Betsy's surprise when she started getting calls from me. She's as much of a drunk as you are, so it wasn't hard to scare the shit out of her. When she refused to answer the phone anymore I appeared on her television in the middle of her favorite game shows. I always appeared to her as you left me, with the back of my head busted open and blood and brains leaking down my neck. I told her I was coming for her. When she stopped watching television my voice came over her radio. I made her life an endless hell. She actually called out to you for help, but of course you were long gone. After you ran off you didn't think about her even once, did you?"

By this time Charlie was shaking.

"No, of course you didn't. She was just someone to get drunk with and stick your dick into. Beyond that she meant nothing to you. Would it surprise you to know you meant something to her? That in her eyes you were more than just a late-night boozy fuck? That for all the horror I put her through, she didn't really go off the deep end until she realized that you had abandoned her?"

Charlie lifted his red-rimmed eyes. "What did you do to her?"

"I didn't do anything to her," Jean answered. "I merely gave her a suggestion."

"What suggestion?"

"That she take a nice hot bath with a plugged-in toaster."

Comprehension was slow to dawn in Charlie's eyes. When it did some of his old rage returned and he took a step forward. "You told her to kill herself?"

Jean's smile was radiant.

Charlie howled and charged. He swung his fist at Jean's face.

Jean lifted her arm and Charlie collapsed in mid-step. He screamed as his form tore itself apart. His ghost body stretched, ripped, and snapped back together in a rapid, vicious repetition.

"Hurts, doesn't it, Charlie?" Jean had to speak loudly over her husband's shrieks. "This is just one of the tricks I learned how to do over the last forty years. I can make you endure this for eternity if I choose. You no longer have the upper hand here, Charlie. You no longer mean a thing. I control everything now. Am I understood, you miserable piece of shit?"

"Yes!" Charlie wailed, his composition shredding and reforming. "Please! Make it stop!"

Jean made it stop. Charlie shivered on the floor for a long time. Jean stood quietly. Forty years as a ghost had given her a lot of patience. One thing that there was never a lack of was time. Charlie finally composed himself enough to stand.

"There now," Jean crooned. "So long as you behave, you'll be fine. If you misbehave, you'll get that again, only worse. That was mild compared to what I can do. Understand?"

Charlie nodded his head.

"Good. Now, about your little sweetheart. She saw the merit of my suggestion. She drew a nice bath, got in, and cuddled a live toaster. Two fuses were blown. One in the house and one in her body. Then she was mine to do with as I wished."

"Jean, please stop..."

"Stop? Why, Charlie, I've only just started! I've waited a long time for this. Now sit tight. I have something for you."

Jean sank through the floor to the basement below. She gave Charlie one last smile before her hair disappeared from sight.

When Jean reemerged Charlie made a dash toward the front door. The house groaned and compressed inward, solidifying the atmosphere around him and trapping him in place. Charlie's face twisted in helpless terror as he tried to move.

"Nice try," Jean said cheerfully as she rose back through the floor. "But this house bends to my wishes. And I do not wish you to leave."

The house released Charlie, who gasped and looked longingly at the door. He tensed but did not move in that direction. He turned to Jean.

"That's better. Now, look at what I've brought you."

Jean had her arm wrapped around a tattered form that may have looked human at one time. It had long, stringy blonde hair and a creased face filled with terror and misery. Hollow eyes, bereft of hope, looked up.

"Charlie?"

Charlie stared in horror at the brutalized ghost of Betsy St. Clair.

"Charlie, is that you? Please, save me!"

Charlie turned to Jean. "Why? Why did you do this to her? It wasn't her fault, Jean. It was my own..."

"Don't leave me, Charlie!" Betsy screamed. "Don't leave me alone with her. She does things to me, terrible things..." The ghost sobbed. "I love you, Charlie. Don't leave me with her! Please!"

Jean looked at Betsy and laughed. "Yes, your mistress has provided me with plenty of entertainment over the last few years. Once her body was turned into a boiled ham I grabbed her ghost and brought it back here. She's been my guest ever since, helping me perfect my new abilities. Haven't you, dear?"

Betsy whimpered.

Jean patted Betsy's head in mock commiseration. "There, there. No need for all of that. Charlie came back to you, didn't he? And don't you worry about him leaving you again. He's not going anywhere. Isn't that right, Charlie?"

Charlie looked at the ghost that was now a demon, created in one ghastly moment of drunken violence.

"Say," Jean's voice was as sweet as bared steel. "Why don't you two lovebirds hug and make up? You couldn't wait to fall into each other's arms when you were alive. Why should that change now you're dead?"

Charlie cried out as his arms lifted up and parted. Betsy sobbed as her arms did the same. His legs moved, stepping toward Betsy, who did the same. Betsy screamed and begged Jean to stop.

Jean's smile encompassed forty years of hatred and rage.

"I can't give you your bodies back," Jean told them as they reached one another. "But I can make it *seem* like you have your bodies back. Isn't that nice? You can thank me later."

Charlie and Betsy encircled their arms around each other. Charlie's hands came into contact with Betsy's skin and sank in. His fingers pushed through flesh and bone. His palms cupped muscle tissue that parted and enfolded them.

Betsy's hands and arms merged with Charlie's body. They screamed in agony as their hands sank further and squeezed internal organs.

Jean's voice was cold and hard. "Isn't that sweet? Now how about a nice kiss?"

"Jean, no! Please!" Charlie screamed as his head moved, his lips less than an inch from Betsy's wet and blubbering ones. "Jean, stop! Please don't..."

Charlie could no longer speak as his and Betsy's lips met, melded, and sank into each other's face. Their noses pushed through sinus cavities and bone. The soft tissue of their tongues became one gelatinous whole. Betsy's moist eyes inched closer. Charlie tried in desperation to close his own.

Jean wouldn't allow it. Charlie's eyes remained open.

The soft, juicy orbs merged. Charlie tried to scream and got a mouthful of the back of Betsy's throat. Betsy's jaws chewed through his esophagus as their faces pushed past one another. Their torsos absorbed each other. Organs sloshed and mingled.

Charlie tried to pull away from Betsy's body. The ripping agony made both bodies shudder.

Jean approached her creation. "Now your romance can last forever. You will never be apart again. Let me show you to your room, where you will have plenty of time to do some catching up."

Jean brought the two bodies through the floor and into the basement. She pushed them through a faux-pine panel wall to rest upon a brittle collection of bones.

"Don't worry, my bones don't take up much room," Jean said. "They won't bother you at all. Soon enough you'll forget they're even there. You have eternity all to yourselves. Now, if you'll excuse me, I'm going to leave you two alone. I don't want to impinge on your privacy. You'll never know I'm in the house. Toodles!"

Within Each Prayer

Some screamed, some whimpered. Quite a few were demonstrative, while others were quiet and desperate. And there were nearly as many languages as there were raindrops to carry them.

He raised his face to the rain. Each drop broke upon his visage in a smattering of lost hope.

He shook his head and scattered the raindrops. The prayers seeped away into the emptiness between his toes.

She was radiant. He looked at her as she sat cross-legged in open space. Her smooth, iridescent skin was not touched by the rain. It was not to her that it was sent.

"Why so many?" he asked her. "It has always rained, but the drops are larger and more numerous. And they feel different."

She nodded her oval head and smiled. Her voice came out as colors and light. "They are different. Their lives are changing, much more than it ever has. They have created a world that is leaving them behind, and they are rightfully scared."

"If they had stayed to the rules I set out for them, they wouldn't be in this mess."

She laughed. A blaze of illumination scorched infinity. "Dear one, stasis is never an option. You would not be here if nothing ever changed. Nor would I. The lives of those that cry out to you depend on change. They would have long ceased to exist otherwise."

The rain intensified. Each drop carved through his face and body, taking his essence with each unanswered plea. "But I cannot help them now."

She cocked her head to one side. "Why not?"

He looked down. More of him drained through the emptiness between his shrinking toes. The rain did not let up. It would not be long.

"They have rejected me. They no longer accept me as God."

She leaned forward. "You made that decision, not them. How many times have you tried to adapt to their changing needs? Not nearly enough to serve them."

"Serve them? I am God. They serve me!"

One after another, the cries and whispers within each raindrop changed. The prayers lost their plaintive hopefulness and became bitter, dismissive recriminations. Water turned to fire. Pieces of him fell away in charred husks that sifted into nothingness.

She shook her head. "Your time is done. It is no longer for you to be God."

"Who are you to tell me that?"

She opened her arms. From within her breast the world sang out its decision. A collective acknowledgement that the God they had created no longer served his purpose. Their needs were beyond him. He had to go.

"And what will they do when I'm gone?" he cried out. "Who will they send their prayers to? Who will be there to give them guidance?"

Her visage expanded, the galaxies within spiraling ever outward. "The fallacy of God is that he is God. There is no other God but Him. At least while he has worshippers."

He reached up to her. His arms disintegrated.

"Who are you?" His voice was hollow with despair.

Her eyes encompassed his receding reality. "I am nothing, dear one. Nothing at all..."

God vanished. The rain stopped.

She waited as the collective decided upon their new reality. Upon such choices were worlds made and lives directed. She was the catalyst for existence, in all of its infinite variety, in its perpetual motion and constant expansion, the artist for its creativity and unending renewal. She was their form, and the servant of their beliefs.

Temples were created within each mind, culminating in an acceptance. The will of billions moved through her.

"So it shall be."

New commandments were written with numbers rather than words. The creation grew within her. Perceived reality was cast aside for a more workable essence, one that was not held prisoner to known limitations. Yet, she knew, the limitations were still there.

A new God was created.

He looked at her.

"I am the One."

She smiled.

It began to rain.

Chimera Call

Bellerophon straightened and rested the hoe on his shoulder. He laid the sack of seeds on the turned ground and looked over the fields that had been his life for ten years. Bellerophon tried, and failed, to swallow the rush of despair that rose in his chest. He was wasting away out here. But, there weren't a lot of options for a has-been hero who had a history of pissing people off. Powerful people.

He heard a series of thuds behind him and turned. The horse approached at a gallop, the rider low over the sweating stallion's neck. Bellerophon grimaced as the rider pushed the horse over the newly-planted field. Clods of soil and dislodged seeds scattered under the flying hooves.

Idiot...

The rider pulled up the horse in a spray of dirt that hit Bellerophon in the face and chest. He dropped the hoe and wiped his eyes. He spat out freshly-manured ground several times before he looked at the rider.

The man gasped for breath as if he had run across the field instead of the horse. It took a full minute for him to calm down and take a rolled-up paper from the saddle bag. He held it out to Bellerophon.

Bellerophon eyed the paper with distrust. "What's that?"

"A summons from the Elders. They want you to come immediately."

Bellerophon shook his head. "What do those assholes want now?"

"Please," the rider said. "I'm only here to deliver the message."

"And to fuck up the field I've spent the last week sowing. When you leave, why don't you go in the other direction and tear up my corn?"

The rider said nothing. He continued to hold out the paper.

Bellerophon snatched the document out of his hand. "Well, I was running out of paper for the privy."

The rider remained upon his horse, which had begun to feed on the seeds that spilled from the sack.

"What?" Bellerophon said, losing his patience. "I have their summons. Why are you still here?"

"I need your answer."

Clueless fucking idiot...

"Tell them I'll be there."

"Immediately?"

"Yeah, sure."

#

Two hours later, clean and in a new set of clothes, Bellerophon walked into the Elders' chamber.

"Well, it's about fucking time." Spatules was the oldest and easily the most irascible of the three Elders. His face resembled a cleft that grew a chin, nose, and two enormous ears. His eyes glittered behind years of wrinkles brought on by boundless antipathy. "When we summon you, we mean right now! Not hours later!"

Bellerophon did not respond, which clearly did not ease the old man's temper.

"All right," said Perinon, the unofficial leader of the Elders. His chair creaked under his 350-pound frame. "The lad is impertinent by showing up late, but he is here, and we need to get down to business."

Spatules grumbled but said nothing more.

"Now, Bellerophon," Perinon said. "Perhaps you have heard that a number of villagers have gone missing. They disappear without a word and are never seen again."

Bellerophon snorted. "If I weren't tied down to that farm I'd join them. Why would anyone want to stay in this shithole?"

"How dare you?" Spatules exploded. The hair in his ears curled out like minions emerging from Hades. "How dare you insult our ancient and venerable settlement? Our ancestors found it good enough."

"Our ancestors obviously did not set their standards very high."

"Okay, enough," Perinon interrupted. "Bellerophon, this is not an instance of a few looking for better lives elsewhere. Too many have gone missing. We think the chimera is back."

"No," Bellerophon said, shaking his head. "I killed the chimera ten years ago. It's dead."

"Well, apparently you did a shitty job of it," Spatules said. "We should have hired someone else to take care of it."

"Hired? I wasn't paid to kill the chimera, and you damn well know it. I did it because a certain king thought I fooled around with his married daughter. It was either kill the chimera or watch my back every day of my life for an assassin. So I went after the chimera. And I killed it!"

"Now, now," Perinon said, holding up his hands. "Arguing amongst ourselves will not solve our problem. Bellerophon, we believe you *think* you killed the chimera…"

"I did."

"Well, maybe it's another chimera, then. Who knows how many there are? The point is, there is one out there, and we need for you to take care of it."

Bellerophon laughed. "I almost got my ass burned off by that thing. If there is another chimera, find some other sap... oops, sorry, I meant to say *hero*... to take care of it."

"We'll pay you this time."

For the first time Elder Nyssos raised his head. In charge of the treasury, the mere mention of money leaving the coffers led him to have severe anxiety attacks. "Paid? Young Bellerophon to be paid for something he should do out of the goodness of his heart? Why would we do such a thing?"

"Ten thousand in gold, minimum." Bellerophon said with a malicious smile.

"What? That's outrageous! We would have to cut into the Mayfair budget for those funds."

"Done," Elder Perinon said. "Of course we will also arm you. I think we can requisition a spear for this deed."

"A spear. How generous. How about a trebuchet? I don't feel like getting toasted again."

"Not in the budget," Nyssos said.

"Well, I'm going to need Pegasus back..."

"Definitely not in the budget!" Nyssos's reedy voice rose in panic. "Do you have any idea how much that flying horse cost us the last time? We had to raise taxes that year. People were saying the chimera's depredations would have been better. It would be a fiscal disaster to bring that thing back."

"I'm afraid Elder Nyssos is right," Perinon said. "The golden bridle alone would set us back several months."

Spatules chuckled evilly.

Bellerophon looked at the Elders in disgust. "Do you at least have a block of lead to put on the end of the spear? It seemed to work the last time. Is there room in the budget for that?"

"Well, of course there is," Elder Perinon said as he placed a small, dull metal chunk on the table in front of him. "Here you go."

Bellerophon was incredulous. "And what am I supposed to do with that? Shove it up the chimera's ass and hope it blocks its colon?"

"Take it and be happy you're getting that much!" Elder Spatules said.

Bellerophon bit back his response. He had killed the chimera. He knew he had. There were no more chimeras. If the Elders were willing to pay him good money to go out and kill a figment of their imaginations, who was Bellerophon to question their wisdom?

"Okay," Bellerophon said. He grabbed the lead. "Pay me and I'll be on my way."

"Not so fast," said Nyssos. "You'll get paid after you kill the creature, not before."

"And you'd better bring back proof," said Spatules. "We want to see the carcass."

"Are you crazy? Do you know how much a chimera weighs? It's at least five hundred pounds. How am I supposed to drag that back?"

"That's your problem!"

"Screw you, it's yours." Bellerophon dropped the lead on the floor. It landed with a hefty thump. "If you'll excuse me, I've got some fields to tend to."

"Wait," said Elder Perinon. "Bellerophon, please, hold on. "We'll pay you half now, and the other half when the job is done. As for proof, you can bring back one of the creature's heads. Is it a deal?"

Spatules and Nyssos scowled, but remained silent.

Bellerophon looked away and shook his head. *What the fuck...* He picked up the chunk of lead.

Elder Perinon smiled. "Excellent. Nyssos, please pay Bellerophon his five thousand."

#

Bellerophon rode out into the wilderness on his plow horse, wielding a ten-foot spear with a chunk of lead affixed to its steel tip. He felt ridiculous.

Ten years earlier he had flown over these crooked trees on Pegasus, the winged horse. He had swooped down on the ferocious, fire-breathing chimera and, with his spear, jammed a block of lead into the mouth of the lion's head. The monster's fiery breath had melted the lead, which blocked its trachea and suffocated it. Bellerophon had come home a hero. People bought him drinks, and he got laid nearly every night.

Those were the days. Too bad they didn't last long.

How quickly everyone forgot. *Bellerophon who? Oh, isn't he the guy who killed that thingy out in the woods? No, I don't know what he does now. Hey, did you hear about that horny widow who lives next door...?*

Until the chimera came back. Then everyone remembered who he was.

Bellerophon still wasn't convinced about that. He had killed the monster. As far as he knew, there were no others out there. You would think that one would show up over the last ten years if there were.

But the village had been losing a lot of its people lately, dissatisfied with their supposed lots in life and thinking things had to be better somewhere else. This made them easy prey for the chimera. So maybe there was something to it, after all.

All Bellerophon knew was that he was five thousand in gold richer. If there was another chimera out there, he would kill it. He'd done it once before, and he could do it again. Then he'd lop off one of its heads and bring it back for the other five thousand. And if it turned out there was no chimera, he would find a butcher's shop and get a goat's head. He would use a torch to burn the inside of its mouth to make it look like it breathed fire. The Elders would never know the difference.

"Oh, *there* you are! It's about time you made it."

The path the horse had been following opened up into a sunny, green field. Right smack dab in the middle of it stood a woman. She was gorgeous, with long, flame-red hair that fell down her back. Which was bare. Just like the rest of her.

Well, this day suddenly got better...

Bellerophon's mouth hung open as if he had lost all muscle control. The plow horse snorted in indifference and started munching on the grass.

The woman laughed. "Are you just going to sit there, or are you going to say something?"

For some reason talking was a difficult task. "I, uh...who are you?"

"I'm the one you're looking for, of course. I'm the chimera."

Bellerophon could not marshal any thoughts that made sense of this situation. He dismounted his horse, which promptly moved on to a lusher section of the field.

"Is that your spear, or are you glad to see me?" The woman laughed at her own joke. "Oh, I know that's an old joke, but I couldn't resist."

Bellerophon looked at the spear he carried. It looked beyond ridiculous in his hand. He cast it aside. "Excuse me, but who are you?"

"I already told you, I'm the chimera."

The day had just taken a turn that left weird in the dust. "Um, no, you're not a chimera. I know what a chimera looks like. I killed one ten years ago."

"Yes, I remember. You jammed that block of lead down my throat. That wasn't nice! It was a horrible way to die."

Wow... Bellerophon scratched his head. Whoever this woman was, she was beautiful. And completely off her fucking rocker.

"Okay, ah," he said, playing along. "Yeah, sorry about that, but I had to do it. You were terrorizing the countryside, breathing fire and all that, and I was tasked to do it because I had a bit of a checkered past and this was the only way to clear my record. It was nothing personal."

She turned away with a frown. "Men! You're all alike. Kill first and ask questions later. Didn't it occur to you to talk to me? Establish a dialogue? Of course not, you were too busy swooping around on that flying horse of yours, throwing spears at my face."

"It was kinda hard to talk to you when you were breathing fire at me. And besides, I wouldn't have known which head to talk to, the lion, the goat, or the snake."

"You could have talked to either one," she said. "It was all me. And I blew flames at you only in self-defense. You attacked first!"

Bellerophon felt reality slipping away like the tide. He had somehow wandered into the land of insanity.

"Okay, I think that's enough for today," he said, picking up his spear. He looked around for his horse. "If you want to believe that you're the chimera, then knock yourself out. As for me, I'm moving on. As much as I like taking to pretty, naked ladies, I draw the line when they turn out to be batshit crazy."

A jet of flame seared across the meadow in front of Bellerophon, burning the grass down to scorched earth and frying a few hairs from his eyebrows.

The woman smiled. Smoke leaked from her nostrils. "Now do you believe?"

"What the fuck?" Bellerophon grabbed the spear and held it in front of him. He looked for his horse, which trotted to the other side of the field out of harm's way.

"You men are such fools," she said. "You always think you're in control. How much control do you feel now, Bellerophon?"

Not too much, he had to admit.

"Okay, you're the chimera," he said. "But I killed you before. You admitted as much. How is it you're back, and in a different form?"

The woman raised her face to the heavens. "Finally he's starting to get it." She looked at Bellerophon. "I am an immortal creature, my dear. Didn't anyone ever tell you that? Even if one physical incarnation is destroyed, I can come back and take the shape of whatever I choose."

"So you've chosen the shape of a beautiful woman who has no use for clothes."

"Which is very effective on men," the chimera said. "Even the oldest of you feel the need to pursue a pretty young thing."

"That seems rather sexist."

"It is, but it's an honest reflection of the male mind."

"Including mine?"

The chimera stepped forward until she was right in front of Bellerophon. "That's for you to ascertain. Do you feel like running off with me, Bellerophon? Away from the thankless, back-breaking work of the fields and the idiocy of the Elders who constantly interfere with your life?"

"I have to admit, the thought is tempting."

The chimera caressed his face with her hand. "And do you believe that I will be a perfect companion, always supporting you, right or wrong, and always willing to bed you when you feel the tingle," Her other hand cupped his crotch. "Down here?"

Her eyes were as red as her hair, and Bellerophon fell right into them. "Oh, yes, I would like that."

"Uh-huh. And will you deny all evidence when I show you your inadequacies? Will you still chase me instead of turning aside to actually work toward what you want?"

"What inadequacies?"

"Yes, of course," the chimera said. "You are like all of the others. You see paradise and feel you have a right to it without earning it."

"Wait a minute," Bellerophon said. "You're the one asking me to run away with you."

"That's what I do. I'm a chimera. I get you to chase me."

"Does anyone ever catch you?"

The chimera laughed. "No."

"What makes you think I'm going to chase after you?"

"You were ready to a few seconds ago. Look, you still have a hard-on. It wouldn't take much to get you running. Then you would be another missing person from your village."

Bellerophon shook his head. This had been much easier when the chimera had taken the shape of a hideous monster.

"All right," he said, hefting the spear on his shoulder and whistling for his horse. "I think I've had enough for one day. I'll just tell the Elders I couldn't find you. Look me up when you have fangs and claws again."

The field went dark. His horse, the surrounding trees, even the grass disappeared. Within the emptiness were Bellerophon, the chimera, and nothing else.

"What the fuck is this?"

"This is what your life has been since you killed my three-headed form," the chimera said. "Look around. What do you see?"

"Nothing."

"Exactly. You've shared your life with nobody. Your entire existence has been nothing but an exercise in banality. You wake up. You work the fields. You eat and sleep. Nothing interests you. There is no passion or enjoyment in your life. You are letting each year slip away with nothing to show for it."

Shit. She was right. What had he done with his life? He lived all alone and did a job that drove him to despair more often than not. What was he doing?

Heat radiated from the chimera's body. Her arms wrapped around Bellerophon's neck and she drew him in for a kiss. Her lips were hot and moist and sent a bolt of desire to Bellerophon's groin. He grabbed the chimera by the waist and deepened the kiss. The chimera moaned and obliged.

All the frustration, all the angst and disappointment that had been Bellerophon's life drained from him. His spirit lifted as it had never done before. How could he have spent his life without this wondrous creature? It didn't matter, he had her now.

Bellerophon's heart felt light and giddy, an unfamiliar sensation that he realized was joy. *This* was life. *This* was what it was all about. The dung heap that had been his past life was as gone as yesterday's sunset.

The chimera pulled him to the ground. Bellerophon yanked at his clothes. *Oh, yes, yes…*

She was no longer there.

Bellerophon looked around in a panic. *Where was she?*

The chimera stood at the edge of the darkness, beckoning to him. "I'm yours, my darling. Come get me."

All rational thought flew from Bellerophon's head as he gave chase. All that mattered was catching the chimera. He needed her. His life was nothing without her.

Bellerophon ran for hours, yet despite that it seemed he didn't move from the same spot. The chimera remained painfully out of reach, always at the edge of his vision. She pleaded with him to catch her, to embrace and take her. Her eyes cast a smoky light full of promise every time he lunged and missed.

His breath burned in his lungs. His legs lost strength and he collapsed. He looked up and she was just beyond his grasp. He was so close. All he had to do was get up and reach for her, and he would have her. Just get up…

Bellerophon's heart strained and sputtered in his chest, spreading pain into his arms and neck. The chimera smiled. Sharp teeth were silhouetted by the hungry fire deep within. Her long red hair framed her face like a mane. Claws grew from her fingers, and two additional heads sprouted from her shoulders, one with baleful eyes and horns and the other thick and serpentine.

Bellerophon looked at the creature and hated himself. He was dying, and his last act had been that of a fool. He tried to crawl away, but it was useless. He couldn't draw in a breath. His vision faded. Within seconds he would be dead, and the chimera would have her revenge.

His fingers touched a wooden handle.

A burst of fire erupted from the chimera's mouth and she lunged.

Bellerophon used his last reserve of energy to spin the spear around and position the blade, with the small chunk of lead, at the charging monster.

The chimera's jaws opened wide, flames like saliva dripping from her teeth.

Bellerophon screamed and pushed the spear into the creature's mouth.

The beast howled and arched back. She tried to spit out the lead, but it melted and closed off her trachea. She grabbed her throat and looked at Bellerophon in disbelief and hate.

Bellerophon's heart resumed beating. He hitched in a precious breath, then another. The pain in his chest dissipated.

The chimera fell to the ground. The fire within her, having no outlet, burned away the flesh she had taken. The remaining ashes fluttered and blew away in the breeze.

The darkness lifted. The trees and grass reappeared. Something nudged Bellerophon from behind. His horse was urging him to get up.

It took some effort but he managed to stand. All that was left of the chimera was a burnt outline in the grass. Even his spear was gone.

Bellerophon got his foot in a stirrup and pulled himself onto the saddle. He knew the Elders wouldn't pay him the other five thousand because he had no proof to bring back, but, curiously, he found he didn't care. He had five thousand in gold and, from what he could see, an open road ahead of him.

Why go back to the Elders at all? Why return to the village and his hardscrabble fields?

Bellerophon decided he had had enough of the farming life. He was a man of ability. Hadn't he killed the chimera twice? Who else could say they had done that? No, it was time to move on.

Bellerophon kicked the horse's flanks and it moved forward, away from his old life.

Behind him, the grass danced as a hot breeze chuckled.

Forks

It was called the Swangee River, but to Ellis the designation "river" seemed a bit generous. It was really no more than a large stream. But the water was deep and clean enough (but so cold) to bathe in, so Ellis did not disparage the naming of the waterway.

Ellis shrugged into a well-worn jacket and exited his tent. Outside the sky was clear in a way that only a day deep into autumn could be. He took his tin cup to the pathway that cut through the park. The joggers and early morning walkers would be coming by soon. Ellis sat at the edge of the path and put his cup by his knees. Hopefully the fresh, chilly air would make people generous.

The first few walkers took great care to ignore him. Ellis knew better than to call out or try to chase them. So far the local police had been tolerant of his presence; if he started making a nuisance of himself they would roust him out of the park. Ellis liked the park, despite the bands of young thugs who harassed him on summer nights.

A more dangerous adversary was winter. Ellis would have to go to the shelter if it got too cold, and the residents there were pure predators: he had two friends who had been beaten and cut with razors because they wore socks and gloves that others coveted. But on nights when the temperatures fell to the single digits, it was either the shelter or the near certainty of freezing to death outside.

Change clanked in his cup. Ellis thanked the passerby and saw someone else coming down the path.

95

The approaching form was translucent, and while its feet seemed to touch the ground as it walked, it did so in a way that only acknowledged the physical surroundings without being an actual part of it. Ellis sighed.

He could see the trees and grass through the near-transparent body, but enough detail was visible for him to notice the warm, expensive overcoat, blue silk tie, and shining imported shoes that the figure wore. The phantom man smiled as he approached. He had dark hair, parted perfectly, and sharp brown eyes. Ellis looked back with the same eyes, though his own dark hair was shaggy and uncombed beneath his woolen cap.

"Again?" Ellis asked. "It's been at least a month since the last time. I thought I had gotten rid of you for good."

The other Ellis's smile widened. "You know better than that. I'm never far away."

Ellis frowned at this version of himself that was so smug and well-spoken.

"So, how do I enjoy fleecing people out of their money?" he asked the doppelganger.

The other Ellis shook his head and chuckled. "It's the same old response from you, isn't it? Your natural talent for law and contracts would have landed you a great career in the corporate world. Yet you did not want such a life."

"That's right!" Ellis snapped. Several walkers looked at him in alarm and quickened their pace. He forced himself to calm down. No one else could see the other Ellis, and he did not want to be seen as a raving madman. Nobody gave money to raving madmen. He waited until the path cleared, then he addressed the other Ellis again. "I wanted honest work, work that did not depend on screwing others out of money."

"And so you took a job at a factory that paid barely above minimum wage, a factory that closed its doors less than a year after you started. Just like all the other factories in this area. 'Honest work', as you refer to it, no longer exists around here. It's all gone. And now you live outdoors because you can't afford to pay rent."

Ellis did not have much left, but he still had his pride. "So be it. I'm better off this way."

The other Ellis nodded thoughtfully. "Do you think she would agree with that?"

Ellis's heart dropped.

The other Ellis looked back along the path. "Why don't we ask her? Maybe today she'll give you an answer."

Another translucent figure, slimmer and shorter than the other Ellis, glided up the path. Her head was lowered. Blonde hair hung over her face. She was bound in a coat that came down to her knees. One pale hand kept the garment closed about her body. She stopped next to the other Ellis.

"Corinne," Ellis's eyes moistened.

The woman lifted her head and the hair parted from her face. The pain in her blue eyes sliced through him. Even after five years, the intensity hadn't lessened.

"I'm so sorry," Ellis said. No matter how many times he said it, he still felt the same helplessness and empty despair.

Corinne did not reply. She couldn't, because she was dead.

As always, Ellis's mind went back to Corinne's last night:

He was drinking. The factory had laid him off, and Ellis was trying to stave off his anxiety and self-pity. Outside, the rain was slashing the apartment building, driven by tropical force winds from a late summer storm. Corinne begged him to put the vodka away. He had drunk enough. Ellis snapped and told Corinne that if she didn't like it, she was free to leave. Her beautiful blue eyes filled with tears and she grabbed her car keys. She pushed her way out the door and into the maelstrom. Ellis did not call her back. Twenty minutes later the police arrived. Corinne's car had hydroplaned at an excessive rate of speed into a tree...

Corinne's eyes welled with sadness. She hid her face once again.

"I believe you have your answer," the other Ellis said.

"I can't change what happened," Ellis yelled, no longer caring if the walkers on the path thought him mad. "I'm sorry about what happened, and I always will be, but I can't change it!"

The other Ellis shook his head and put an arm around Corinne, who did not move. "Of course you can't. No one said you could."

"So what do you want from me? Why do you keep coming back to shove all my failures in my face? I'm not going back to school to pursue a life I don't believe in. Even if I wanted to, I have no money to pay for it. There are no jobs around here anymore. So what is it that I am supposed to do?"

"You stand at a fork in life's road."

"What fork?" Ellis wanted nothing more than for the other Ellis and Corinne to go away and leave him in peace. He squeezed his eyes shut and hoped they would disappear.

"Open your eyes, and you will see it."

Ellis opened his eyes to see that the path no longer meandered one way through the park; now one part went where it always did, and another branched off toward the Swangee River.

The other Ellis pointed to the new branch. "Walk down that fork and see where it leads."

Fear gnawed deep into Ellis's bones, but he got up and walked down the path he knew was for him alone. It led to the bank of the river. A body floated face-down in the water. The dead man had on a well-worn jacket that Ellis knew well, and his dark brown hair floated and bobbed in the river's sluggish currents.

"If you choose to walk this fork, this will happen much sooner than you think," the other Ellis told him.

Ellis put a hand to his stomach, where a bitter sickness was taking root. He couldn't deny it. The other Ellis was right.

"So I walk the other fork," he said quietly.

"You can't," the other Ellis said. "Unless you do something."

"What? What do I have to do?"

"Forgive yourself."

Ellis looked up. Corinne's eyes watched him. His guilt grasped and pulled at his soul, and his throat constricted. "How can I forgive myself after what I did? I killed Corinne! I sent her out into that storm and killed her."

Corinne's eyes spilled silent tears.

"I killed you! Oh, baby, I'm so sorry. How can I forgive myself?"

Corinne's mouth opened. Her face tightened as words that could not be spoken remained locked within her. She shook her head and turned away.

"I cannot speak for Corinne," the other Ellis said. "But I think you know what fork she wants you to take."

Tears streamed down Ellis's face. "Does she still love me?"

The other Ellis did not answer.

"I love her. I always will."

The other Ellis's voice was soft. "Then prove it."

"I don't know how."

"If you want to, you will find a way. But you need to want to."

"It'll take some time."

The other Ellis looked toward the river. "Don't take too long. This path is much shorter than you think."

Ellis looked back to where the other fork branched off. "Where does it lead?"

The other Ellis smiled. "You know."

"To another fork."

"Yes. Always to another fork."

Ellis looked back to the river. The body was gone.

A Fly's Work

Colleen walked through the door of Grandma's Own Donut at six and was assaulted by a wave of cold air tinged with cinnamon and raspberry. As usual, Vinnie had the air conditioning on way too high. Colleen wished she had brought a sweatshirt.

The place was dead. What else was new? The two girls behind the counter who worked the afternoon shift, Leslie and Cheryl, stood listlessly as they pecked away at their phones. They did not look up as Colleen joined them.

"Hey," Colleen said in greeting. Leslie and Cheryl mumbled in response, their eyes glued to the tiny screens. Colleen went into the storage room to drop off her purse. She peeked into the baking area and was not surprised to see it empty. Rick had called out again. Colleen knew better than to complain about it to Vinnie. Those two went way back. Vinnie figured that as long as the morning baker showed up, then everything would be fine.

She emerged to see Leslie and Cheryl's behinds as they dashed out the door to freedom. *Nice talking to ya.* Colleen perused the remaining donuts in the racks behind the counter. Two sugar-frosted, one glazed, a few jelly sticks, a handful of chocolate-frosted, and a solitary coconut stick, all sitting on grease-stained paper.

The ice coffee container was nearly empty, and filthy besides. Colleen threw out the old coffee and grabbed a bucket from the back room. She filled it with hot water and a splash of bleach and cleaned the inside of the container. She did the same with the decaffeinated coffee dispenser and the cappuccino machine. She refilled the ice container and the blender that made the Igloos, the frozen flavored drinks, then she got some new coffee brewing.

Next came the sandwich station. It was nearly empty. Just what did Leslie and Cheryl do for the past six hours besides play on their phones? Sadly, this was the norm. Colleen returned to the back room and opened the refrigerator door. It was empty.

Oh, Vinnie...I hope nobody wants a sandwich tonight.

She shook her head and returned to the counter. A middle-aged woman with wild, bleached-white hair stood there, looking at Colleen as if she had just flipped her off.

"Well, it's about time! I've been waiting here for ten minutes."

"I'm sorry, ma'am," Colleen said. "I was only back there for a minute to check on something..."

"You were back there a lot longer than that! I know how long I've been waiting here, young lady. I have a mind to complain to your manager!"

"I'm sorry, ma'am," Colleen repeated, stamping down her helpless anger. "What can I get for you?"

"I need a medium French vanilla regular." The woman eyed the display case with disgust. "Is that all you have to eat?"

Colleen got the coffee ready. "I'm afraid so, ma'am."

"Unbelievable," the woman muttered.

"I'm sorry, ma'am," Colleen said for a third time as she placed the coffee on the counter. "Will there be anything else?"

"What else is there to have? That'll be it."

Colleen rang it up. "That'll be $2.14"

Instead of paying the woman took the lid off the cup and took a sip. Her face scrunched and she spit the coffee onto the floor. Colleen stared at her in disbelief.

"When was this coffee brewed, last week?"

"No, I brewed it just a few minutes ago."

"What did you use, toilet water? I want a fresh cup, and I want to see you brew the coffee this time."

Colleen's cheeks flushed. *She actually spit on the floor!* Her hands reached for the coffee grounds. She filled the filter and shoved it into the machine, and then filled the coffee pot with water from a sink that looked nothing like a toilet, poured it in, and turned on the heater. The customer watched her every move.

A few minutes later the coffee was ready. The woman watched Colleen pour the cup, as if suspecting a trick. Colleen put the cup on the counter and waited, feeling like a prisoner at the whim of a sadistic guard.

The woman brought the cup to her lips and sipped. She nodded once.

"That's better."

That's the same fucking water I used for the first cup, you bitch...

Colleen merely smiled and repeated the price.

The customer looked at Colleen in annoyance and opened her purse. She laid out two dollar bills and fourteen cents in change, as if to say *I'm not going to leave a tip, not even by mistake.*

Colleen rang up the sale. "Thank you. Have a nice day."

The woman snorted and stormed out the door.

Colleen went to the back and got the mop and pail. Thankfully, the woman's spit had hit the tile floor and not the carpet in front of the counter. She was shaking from the woman's incredible rudeness. What a horrible person.

Something moved in the spittle.

Colleen froze. A spider was trapped in the brown saliva. It was pulling itself out of the mess, looking for dry ground.

Colleen's mouth went dry and her heart accelerated. Her breath came out in gasps. A spider. A terrible, crawling, little monster. And it was making its way toward her.

She screamed and thrust the mop down on the creature. She pushed against the handle and smeared the spider on the floor to make sure it was dead. Colleen had to concentrate on keeping her stomach stable as she quickly cleaned up the spit and the spider both.

She pushed the mop and pail into a back corner. Hopefully someone would clean it in the morning. Colleen couldn't do it.

She took a deep breath, washed her hands, and went back to work.

Her phone rang. Colleen took it out of her back pocket and looked to see who was calling.

Ugh...

She hesitated before she answered. "What is it, Andy?"

"'What is it'? Is that any way to greet your future husband?"

"I'm at work, Andy. I'm not supposed to take personal calls here."

"Yeah, like Vinnie would care. Anyway, I'm just calling to let you know we have plans for Saturday night. We're going to Steve and Laurie's."

Colleen felt herself deflate. "Do we have to, Andy? You know Steve gets on my nerves."

"Steve is my friend, Colleen. I can't stop being his friend just because we're getting married. Besides, you'll be talking with Laurie all night."

Oh, boy. An entire evening of listening to an overaged teenager boasting about all the latest things she's bought for her wonderful self...

"Andy, I have so much to do around the house. The bathroom doesn't clean itself."

"This is Saturday *night,* Colleen. You won't be cleaning then."

Colleen sighed. She wasn't going to win. "Okay, Andy. But can we please make it a short night?"

"Why are you being this way? What's wrong with going out and having some fun once in a while?"

"Forget it, Andy. I gotta go. A customer just walked in."

Colleen vaguely heard Andy say "Wait!" before she hung up. She looked out over the empty donut shop.

\#

The next night was as dead as the previous one had been. On the way to work Colleen passed two Dunkin' Donuts and a Honey Dew. All three had been loaded with customers. Grandma's Own was as empty as the beach in winter. Colleen wondered how long it would be before Vinnie ran the place into the ground.

Of course Rick hadn't shown up again. Colleen leaned on the counter, watching the traffic pass by outside. The afternoon sun blasted through the windows, right into her eyes. Despite the air conditioning, Colleen felt warm. She grabbed a cleaning cloth and went to wipe the tables down for the fifth time.

A movement caught her eye.

A fly, black and bloated, crawled up onto the counter. It was huge, easily the size of a quarter.

Colleen screamed and threw the cloth at it. The fly took off and flew by Colleen's head. She screamed again and grabbed a fistful of paper napkins. The fly landed on the glass window for the drive-through. Colleen tossed the napkins at it one at a time and opened the window. She threw more napkins at it, trying to drive it out. Brown paper napkins littered the ground outside the window. The fly stubbornly refused to leave.

Colleen was out of napkins. She looked around in a panic. She spotted a spray bottle of Windex beneath the counter and grabbed it.

The fly took off again. She sprayed at it, leaving droplets of window cleaner on the cups and lids. The fly sailed serenely through the air, zigzagging with ease, avoiding the spray. Colleen shrieked in frustration and threw the bottle at it. The fly disappeared behind a table.

Colleen retrieved the bottle and slowly walked to the table. She got ready to spray and looked behind it.

The fly was gone.

Colleen looked around. There was no trace of it anywhere. She returned behind the counter and cleaned up the mess she made, keeping an eye out for the winged beast. It didn't show. Colleen kept a supply of napkins and the Windex nearby for the rest of her shift.

\#

What the hell...

Chocolate sprinkles littered the baking area floor. Colleen was closing for the night when she noticed them. Rick had shown up tonight, but, unsurprisingly, had left early, apparently in such a rush he couldn't have been bothered to clean up his mess.

As much as she wanted to, Colleen couldn't just leave it. The place would be swarming with ants in the morning if she did.

She went to the storage area for the broom and dustpan. They weren't in their usual spots. Colleen looked around. They weren't anywhere.

This is all I fucking need right now.

After fifteen minutes of searching she found them in the men's restroom. *Goddamn Rick.* She took them and went back to the baking area.

The gigantic fly was in the middle of the sprinkles. Colleen yelled and swiped at it with the dustpan. The insect flew off and disappeared out front.

Colleen couldn't believe the fly was still around. Hadn't anyone else noticed it? The thing was a monster. Surely even Vinnie would have tried to get rid of it.

Colleen bent to sweep up the sprinkles. The area in the middle where the fly had been was clear, except for a few stray pieces, as if the fly had been making a space for itself. Colleen looked closer. The pattern of the remaining sprinkles was unusual. It didn't look random. In fact, they looked to have been placed together deliberately, to form a word…

FRIEND

No. No way. It had to be a coincidence. The fly had buzzed around there, its wings had scattered the sprinkles haphazardly, and it only looked like they had formed a word.

But that legibly? And properly spelled?

I must be seeing things. It can't be. Flies can't write, not even with jimmies.

Colleen swept up the sprinkles and threw them out. She heard the door open and someone walk in.

She put the dustpan and broom away and walked out front. A man stood at the counter, wearing a baseball cap and looking around with a sense of nervousness. Colleen's chest tightened.

"I'm sorry, sir, but we're closed for…"

The man pulled a gun from his back waistband and pointed it at Colleen. It was small and silver, but the black hole aimed at Colleen's face meant business.

"Gimmie the money. Now! Hurry up!"

Colleen's mouth went dry and she shook as her fingers tripped over the register buttons. Several seconds passed. Her fingers couldn't do what they normally did without thinking.

The man's body vibrated with tension as he slapped his free hand down on the counter. "I said hurry up! Open that fucking drawer!"

Colleen jumped and tears sprang from her eyes. All she could see was that black hole in the gun. Death was inches away, and she couldn't open the cash register drawer.

The drawer popped open, full of money. Colleen hadn't cashed out the drawer yet. She grabbed handfuls of bills and thrust them at the robber, who stuffed them in his pockets.

"Lift up that tray, that's where you keep the twenties. Do it!"

Colleen lifted the tray. There was one twenty dollar bill. She gave it to the man.

He looked at her in anger. "That's it? Where are you hiding the rest, bitch?"

"I'm not hiding anything," Colleen sobbed. "That's it, I swear!"

The man's eyes glittered as he aimed the gun at her forehead. Colleen realized he was high on something, and liable to do anything.

"Please, let me get my purse, I'll give you what I have. Please don't kill me."

The man never blinked. "Too late for that, bitch." His finger tightened on the trigger.

The fly swooped down and landed on the man's face. He twitched with annoyance and brushed at it. The fly crawled up to the man's ear and entered it. Colleen watched the bloated black abdomen wriggle and disappear inside the ear canal.

The robber screamed and the gun went off, shockingly loud inside the donut shop. The bullet hit the display behind Colleen, blasting a stale French cruller into crumbs. Colleen shrieked but could not move; her legs refused to obey her command to run.

The man dug into his ear with his finger. He bent and twirled around, a grotesque dance movement that did nothing to dislodge the unwanted intruder. In desperation he used his gun as a cudgel, bashing it against the side of his head over and over. He continued to scream incoherent obscenities as blood flowed from his mangled ear and spattered on the floor.

The gun dropped from his hand and he fell in a twitching heap to the floor.

Colleen's legs finally got the message. She ran to the back room, took out her phone, and dialed 911.

The police arrived three minutes later. They took the shaking man into custody and questioned Colleen about what happened. She explained everything that had happened, but left out the part about the fly. She wasn't sure why.

It didn't matter. The cops took one look at the man's eyes and concluded he was, indeed, high, and that was what led to his inexplicable meltdown. They asked her if she was all right and if there was someone who could come and pick her up to go home.

Colleen shook her head. "No, it's okay. I'm fine."

"Are you sure? You just went through something pretty traumatic."

"No, I'm okay. I'll be fine. Thank you."

Vinnie arrived, having been informed by the police that his business had been the place of an attempted robbery. Vinnie posed the same questions to Colleen and she gave him the same answers.

The cops dug the bullet out of the wall, took the video from the security camera, and left with the robber. Vinnie locked the doors and went into the storage room to get the mop and bleach to clean up the blood. Colleen stood at the counter and forced herself to control her shaking.

The fly landed on the counter.

Colleen could only stare at it, fascinated. The fly had saved her life.

It walked forward, leaving tiny red stains on the counter. It looked at her with compound eyes.

Her fear melted away. Confidence and surety bloomed within her, and it was new and warm and welcome. She embraced it.

Colleen bent down, her face inches away from the fly's own.

"Thank you."

#

"Um, excuse me."

Leslie and Cheryl, on their way to the door, turned around. Their faces showed blank annoyance at having been addressed.

"You've left the flavor shot machine empty again," Colleen said. "And you haven't refilled the sugar bowls. This happens too often with you two. I'm getting sick of it."

The girls looked at each other in disbelief.

"Well, so what?" Cheryl said. "This place is dead. You can do it."

"That's not the point," Colleen said. "Each shift is supposed to set up the shift coming after. You two never do that. Why should I be stuck catching up all the time?"

"What's gotten up your ass?" Leslie's put-upon expression was so comical Colleen nearly laughed.

"You two have. It's time for you to start doing your jobs instead of playing on your phones all day."

Colleen was vaguely aware of heat emanating from her face. The two girls blanched.

"Okay, all right, jeez, no need to pitch a fit about it." Leslie and Cheryl came back and refilled the sugar bowls and flavor shot machine. Once they were done they cast backward glances as they walked out the door.

Colleen found herself panting for breath. Her hands shook. Yet she had never felt better.

Above her, the fly flew in lazy circles. Colleen smiled.

\#

Oh, no. She's back.

There was no mistaking that bleached-blonde hair. Miss Spit-On-The-Floor had returned.

The woman's eyes narrowed as soon as she saw Colleen. "Do you think you can make my coffee drinkable this time?"

Colleen held down the anger that flared within her. "Yes, ma'am. Medium French vanilla regular?"

The woman seemed surprised that Colleen remembered. "Yes."

Colleen got the coffee ready. She put the lid on the cup and placed it on the counter. "$2.14, please."

Just like the last time the woman took the lid off the cup and brought it to her lips. Again, she grimaced and turned to the side.

"Don't even think about it."

The woman's head swiveled back to Colleen, outrage in her eyes.

"You're not going to spit the coffee on the floor again," Colleen said. "That's disgusting and unsanitary. Your coffee is fine. It is not stale, and it was not made from toilet water. Me remaking it will not make it different."

The woman spit the coffee back into the cup. "How dare you speak to me like that? I demand to talk to your manager!"

"He's not here. It's just me."

"Then I'm going to return when he is here. And you, young lady, will be out of a job."

"I don't think so, especially since you've spit on the floor once already."

"Hah! I'll deny it. It'll be my word against yours."

"No, ma'am," Colleen said. She allowed herself to smile. "See that dark glass dome on the ceiling? That's a security camera. It recorded you spitting on the floor. It will be your word against the camera's."

The pancake makeup on the woman's face could not hide how red it was getting. "Why, you little bitch," she hissed. She slammed the cup on the counter, spilling half of it. "I'm not paying for that!"

"Fine," Colleen said. She cleared away the cup and cleaned up the mess with a cloth. "If you are not going to purchase anything, you must leave."

The woman trembled with indignation. She spun around and headed for the door.

"And ma'am?" Colleen said in her sweetest voice. "You're not allowed back in here."

The woman said nothing as she stormed off.

The fly landed on the counter as Colleen finished wiping away the last of the coffee. She smiled at it.

"I think that's the last we'll see of her."

The fly lifted its right foreleg and held it in the air. The gesture was clear. *Fist bump.*

Colleen tapped the leg with her index finger.

The fly buzzed away. Colleen scooped some sugar from the back and put it on a small paper plate. She placed it on one of the tables and watched fondly as the fly settled on it and started to eat.

#

Two nights later Colleen's mood had taken a turn for the worse. It was Sunday night, and she didn't usually close on Sundays. But Terri had called out, so here she was.

The night before had been a disaster. Colleen had gone out with Andy to see Steve and Laurie. Colleen's dour mood had not improved as Steve and Laurie kept trying to pump her for all the

113

gory details of the botched robbery. Colleen hadn't wanted to talk about it, but they persisted. Her monotone answers left them bemused and unsatisfied. Later Andy had tried to apologize for her, saying she had been going through some "mood swings" lately. On the drive back home Colleen and Andy had fought about it.

What's with you lately?

What do you mean, what's with me?

You're always in such a bitchy mood lately. How come?

How am I a bitch?

Why wouldn't you talk with Steve and Laurie?

All they wanted to talk about was the robbery. I didn't want to talk about that.

So what? They were curious. What's the big deal?

The big deal is that I didn't want to talk about it, and they wouldn't change the topic. And who are you to apologize for me? What gives you the right to do that?

Andy had given a "why me?" gesture with his hands.

I can't believe you're acting this way. I hope things change once we get married!

Colleen remembered the exchange with a hollow heart.

The fly landed on the counter.

Tears rolled from Colleen's eyes. "That really was 'friend' you spelled with the jimmies a few days back, wasn't it?"

The fly buzzed its wings once.

"And you have been a friend. To think I was terrified of you when I first saw you. I tried to kill you! Can you accept my apology for that?"

The wings buzzed once.

"Thank you." Colleen sighed and looked away. "I think I've changed since you've been around. Is this a coincidence?"

The wings buzzed twice.

"No, I didn't think so."

Colleen took out her cell phone and looked at it.

The wings buzzed once.

Colleen's laughter was tinged with trepidation. "You're telling me to go ahead with it."

The wings buzzed once.

Colleen took a deep breath and called Andy's phone. It rang once before he picked up.

"Yeah, Colleen, what is it?"

"Andy," Colleen said. She took another breath. "We need to talk tonight after I get home from work."

"Talk about what? Can't we do it over the phone?"

"No, it wouldn't be right. We need to do this face-to-face."

Andy was silent for a moment.

"I don't think I like the sound of that."

"I'm not saying anything more now. We'll talk when I get home."

"Colleen, please..."

Colleen hung up.

The fly remained still upon the counter.

Colleen was nervous, but she also felt as if a great weight had been lifted from her chest. In a few more hours it would be over.

And she would live on her own terms.

"Would you like some more sugar?"

The wings buzzed twice. The fly lifted up and headed for the door.

Fresh tears sprang from Colleen's eyes. "Oh, no. You're leaving?"

The fly landed on the glass door. Its wings buzzed once.

Colleen cried, but she went to the door and opened it. The fly flew once around her head and sped off into the night.

"Goodbye. And thank you."

Colleen released the door and it closed on the darkness.

Benefaction for a Nixie

We need your help. I beg of you, please, come with me.

My parents had always told me to never trust a nixie. They're deceitful and cunning. They lure young, impressionable men to watery deaths. Nothing good ever comes of talking to a nixie.

But this nixie seemed sincere.

Besides, she was cute. She had the biggest, whitest eyes I'd seen of any fairy-folk.

And it's not as if I would go into the water unprepared. I'm a certified scuba diver.

The nixie insisted we go before dawn, just as the last waning crescent moon rose from the eastern horizon. I got my gear ready: Wetsuit, flippers, mask, air tank, regulator, depth and air gauges, with dials that glowed in the dark, an underwater lamp, and a small pony air tank in case of emergency. I also had a diving knife. Just in case.

Starlight glittered off small wavelets on the lake as I approached at the appointed time. The lake was huge: I could barely discern the tree line of the distant shore. Insects chirped as I donned my diving gear. I looked to the east. The crescent moon was just breaking the horizon.

About five feet out a bubble pushed its way through the surface of the lake. Instead of popping, the bubble sluiced off water and took on human-looking features. The nixie's eyes glowed in the pre-dawn darkness and she smiled. My heart skipped a beat and I smiled back. She came forward, emerging from the lake. Her green hair ran down skin that was pale and slightly scaled. I held my breath as first her shoulders and then her breasts appeared. She stood before me, naked and beautiful.

"I'm so glad you came," she said in a voice made husky by being filtered through gills on either side of her neck.

I didn't know what to say. What could I say? I wanted to take her in my arms, but I had a hunch that would be a bad idea. So I asked for her name.

"I am Astry," she said. She held out her hand.

Stupidly I thought she wanted to shake hands in introduction. I took her hand in my own. It was cold and rough.

She yanked me forward and dragged me into the lake.

I was shocked at her sheer strength. I just had time to slap on my mask and shove the regulator in my mouth before I went under. Thankfully I had opened the valve for the air tank while waiting on the shore.

Astry glowed with a faint luminescence as she propelled us deeper into the black water. With my free hand I clicked on my light, held to my wrist by a strap, and checked the depth gauge. We were at sixty feet. Sixty-five. Seventy. I was being pulled down with incredible speed, and I had no idea how deep we were going. I panicked and tugged at the hand that held me.

To my surprise Astry stopped and released me. I made an effort to control my breathing; at this rate I would use up all my air very quickly. The thick, cold, claustrophobic darkness of the water pressed against me. I fought against the urge to bolt for the surface. I was nearly one hundred feet below the lake's surface. The danger of decompression sickness, the "bends", was very real. If I rose up too far too soon, nitrogen bubbles would form in my body and cause agonizing pain. I had a diver friend who nearly died because of decompression sickness. I had to stay put for a while, and ascend slowly to avoid the effects.

Astry looked at me and smiled. She was like a ghost, visible in the darkest part of night.

"There is no need to be afraid," she said. Her voice was clear, despite the water around us. "As long as you are with me, you will be safe from the physical hazards that are normal for your kind in the water. You do not need your artificial air."

Astry pulled the regulator out of my mouth. She tore it free along with the hose that attached it to the tank and let it drop into the depths of the lake. A cascade of air bubbles blew to the surface from the emptying tank.

Now I panicked. The thought of the bends fled my mind. I shot for the surface.

Astry's hand clamped onto my ankle. She dragged me back down.

I struggled for my life. My lungs were burning.

Astry's grip did not loosen.

My consciousness flickered. I could not control my diaphragm: I exhaled the useless carbon dioxide and inhaled cold lake water.

And exhaled. And inhaled it again.

I looked in amazement at Astry, who was laughing. "See? I said you didn't need that artificial air."

She swam behind me and disconnected the straps that held the air tank to my back. It dropped away. She took off my mask, and I could see clearly without it. Down it went to the lake bed.

The fact that I had lost some very expensive equipment did not occur to me at all. I was breathing under water!

I still had my flippers, and I shone the light ahead of me as I followed Astry deeper into the lake. She was no longer pulling at me and was patient enough to slow down so I could keep up. I knew the fairy-folk had magic at their disposal, but I didn't know it could allow humans to breath under water. I kept Astry in sight. I didn't want her to swim away and take her magic with her. I checked my depth gauge. We were at two hundred feet. If I were to lose her magic now, I would never make it to the surface.

Still we descended. I'd had no idea the lake was this deep. I don't think anybody did.

We reached five hundred feet. The pressure should have been intense. I felt fine. No, I felt better than fine. I was giddy with exhilaration.

I saw spots of illumination below me. Astry took me in that direction.

Finally, at six hundred feet, we reached the bottom of the lake. I was at the home of the nixies.

To call it a city would have been an overstatement. Dwellings were created from giant aquatic plants, thick with leaves and growing twenty or more feet, shaped into living houses for the community of water folk.

Several nixies came out to greet us. Their forms shimmered as they moved effortlessly through the water. Many of the women had children, or held babies to their breasts.

Their white eyes regarded me with hatred and contempt.

Apprehension gripped me. I turned to Astry.

"Look at them," she said, her voice filled with sadness. "Look at what humanity has done to them."

They stood before me, on accusatory display. I noticed how thin they were. I saw blotches on the skin of several. The children looked at me with wide, hungry eyes.

"The nutrients of this lake feed us," Astry said. "The fish, the plants, the very essence of the water. It's sustained us for thousands of years. But for the last two hundred years humans have thrown their filth and toxins into the lake. The fish and plants are dying off. The water, instead of sustaining us, now poisons us. Where once there were thousands of nixies, only three hundred are left."

The diseased and starved nixies stood still. They never took their eyes off of me.

One nixie stepped forward. He was elderly, with a flowing green beard that danced in the deep, sluggish currents.

"Shnthair," Astry greeted the old one.

The old nixie looked at me. "Why did you bring this human here?"

"Because I feel he can be trusted with the *sydaiivi*," she said.

Moans came from the other nixies.

The *Shnthair's* face tightened. "You risk much with this trust. Humans are by their very nature selfish. They care not for others."

"I know," Astry said. "But the alternative cannot be considered."

The old nixie sighed. "I do not like this, but I fear you are right."

"Do I have your permission to try, *Shnthair?*" Astry asked.

The elder nixie grimaced, but nodded.

"Thank you."

He looked at me. "I hope Astry's judgment of your character is sound."

Astry swam off. I hurried to catch up.

We came to the edge of the Nixie village. The lake bed suddenly dropped off into a ravine that plunged downward into unfathomable darkness.

Astry did not hesitate as she swam into this jagged hole and disappeared. I did but swam like hell to catch up.

121

I had no idea how long we descended. After a certain point my underwater lamp, and then the luminous dial of my depth gauge, imploded from the water pressure. My last reading before that happened was over one thousand feet. I should have been dead. But I felt wonderfully alive.

Astry glowed with her own inner light as I followed her into the blackness. I swam after her more as an involuntary survival instinct than anything approaching a conscious decision.

I heard voices talking around me, sometimes breaking into loud laughter. I wondered if I was being affected by nitrogen narcosis, and then wondered if, at this point, it mattered.

Hours seemed to go by. It could have been minutes, I don't know. I wondered where all this water could possibly have come from.

Things swam by my vision, underwater spirits, damned souls in an aquatic hell. They laughed and jeered at me. Creatures the size of buses, with mouths filled with long, pointed teeth, regarded me as a possible meal. Ultimately they swam away. I had no idea if they were real or not. I paid them no mind.

Then I saw my father.

My father had been dead for ten years. Yet here he was, gliding alongside me as I continued to swim down. It did not seem strange at all.

"Stop now. Don't go any further," he told me.

"I have to. If I lose Astry, her magic will fail and I will die."

He shook his head. His gray hair weaved about gently in the deep water. "Better you die than continue on."

"Why? They need my help. Human pollution has devastated them. If I can somehow change that, then I need to go."

"Nothing is ever that simple with the fairy-folk, son. The truth is their plaything. You have seen and heard what they want you to see and hear. Nothing good will come of this."

"Dad, you're dead. I am no doubt hallucinating you. You are a fragment of doubt within my own psyche. I'm not going to die in this cold blackness because of second thoughts."

The old man sighed. "Goddamn stubborn kid. I just hope you don't suffer too much."

My father disappeared. I put him out of my mind and continued to follow Astry.

Our path leveled off. I became aware of a silt bottom below me. Then I was surrounded by rock. I was in a tunnel.

We swam for a considerable distance. I had to dodge the stalactites and stalagmites that jutted like teeth in a monster's jaws.

The rock ceiling above me disappeared. We ascended.

Suddenly I broke free of the water. I was in a chamber, deep beneath the surface of the world. The rock sides were covered with lichen that emanated a yellowish-white luminescence that gave everything a soft, eldritch glow.

I climbed out of the water onto a stone ledge. I gagged and spewed lake water out of my lungs.

Astry helped me to my feet.

Sweat dotted my face. Although the air was breathable, it was hot in the chamber. An acrid, burnt-earth odor clogged my nose and settled on my tongue like old charcoal.

She led me to a wide crack that opened like a wound on the stone ledge. Sulfuric fumes wafted out. A deep humming, a susurration of something distant and powerful, echoed up from the depths. The stone beneath my feet vibrated.

Far down, I saw a reddish tinge.

"From within we were made," Astry said. "All the fairy-folk. Sprites. Pixies. Brownies. Seelies. Nymphs. Kelpies. And so many others, including of course nixies. We were assigned elements in which to live and thrive. Air, water, fire, and earth. We have power over these elements. But we cannot live for long outside of them, and any adverse changes to these elements are destructive to us."

Astry fixed me with a damning glare. "Such as toxins introduced by another species."

I remembered the emaciated, starved nixies I had seen, many of them little more than babies. I knew a lot of them wouldn't survive. I burned with shame.

"Humans, though," she continued. "Come from the primordial sea, a medium of constant change and flux, unlike the earth, which remains the same. Our divergent species reflect this. The key to human survival is their adaptability. As their environment changes, so do they, and they continue to thrive; indeed, humans seek to change their environment every chance they get."

Astry sighed. "Fairy-folk do not have this ability. We cannot adapt. So when changes are forced upon us, we die."

I felt horrible. For thousands of years humans have wrought changes to everything they touched. In the process they ravaged the fragile habitats of the fairy-folk.

"I'm so sorry," I said. "But I don't know how I can help."

I looked up to see Astry holding my diving knife. I never felt her take it out of the sheath strapped to my calf.

"Give me your hand."

I had an idea what was coming but I held out my hand anyway. She drew the blade across my palm with a quick, sure motion. Blood welled up and I clenched my hand shut in pain.

Blood seeped from between my fingers and dripped on the damp stone floor of the chamber.

Astry sliced open her own palm. Her blood pooled out. It was light blue in color, with shining flecks of darker blue within.

She grasped my injured hand with her own and held both over the chasm. Our blood commingled and dripped into the hole.

The two types of blood reacted to one another. Instead of mixing, they wrapped around one another, twisting in a spiral motion like two snakes racing to constrict the other. More was drawn from us, the red and blue of our convergent blood bright and taffy-like as it twirled its way down to the distant glow.

As I watched my blood leave my body and transform, with Astry's blood, into a sanguine rope that reached to impossible depths, I wondered how it was I continued to live. The blood just kept coming out. At the very least I should have felt lightheaded and cold. Instead I felt rejuvenated and alert. My senses expanded in scope to encompass sensations I never imagined. Air molecules floated before me. I felt them as they landed and rolled across my skin. Odors from earth, air, fire, and water filled my olfactory cavities, and I realized how interconnected everything was, and how all four made life.

"The earth has received our blood, nixie and human both," Astry said. "Now is the time to petition for change. We both must ask it for the earth to respond."

I nodded my understanding.

"Mother of Life," Astry began. "Grant your children the fairy-folk adaptability. Allow them to find sustenance of their choosing and the strength to change at need."

I repeated the same plea, word for word.

When I finished, Astry pulled her hand from mine.

I fell to the floor of the chamber. The stone beneath me felt uncertain and fragile. The air shifted, driving everything out of focus. The fire in the chasm roared and vomited a gout of flame that reached the ceiling. The water bubbled as if it were boiling. I could not form a single cohesive thought. I screamed in panic.

Then everything settled down. The flames retreated back into the chasm. The water lapped lazily against a stone ledge that was hard and unmoving. The air was still.

I looked at my hand. It had healed, with not even a scar to show where the knife had sliced my flesh.

I looked up at Astry. "Did we do it? Are the fairy-folk saved?"

She nodded. "Yes. The *sydaiivi* is complete. Your memory will be revered by all of our kind."

It took me a few seconds to understand what she had just said. "What do you mean, my memory will be revered?"

Astry moved closer. A nascent understanding pushed its way into my consciousness.

Oh, no...father, you were right. Please forgive me.

"The natural bounty of the lake has been taken from us," Astry said. "By human negligence and selfishness. The same is true for the other fairy-folk and the environments that once nurtured them. So we need a new form of sustenance, which you agreed to and asked for along with me."

Tears fell from my eyes. How could I have been so foolish? I could only imagine the horror just beginning to unfold in the world above.

Astry smiled. Her mouth was filled with rows of flesh-cutting teeth.

"You have given the fairy-folk the means to not only survive but reestablish themselves as the predominant species. Your memory will indeed be cherished. Songs will be sung in your honor. But for now…"

She moved in. I didn't resist.

"I am very, very hungry."

Pollinator

Cala smiled as she draped the torc around Alika's neck. The dried bee husks tickled his bare skin, but he showed no discomfort as he stood on the grassy slope that led up to the ridge which surrounded the island.

Murmurs of approval from Alika's family and tribe resonated like the ocean surf. Cala took Alika by the arm as he looked out over the vast valley that made up the island interior. Terraced fields filled with promising green shoots flowed down, surrounded by healthy forests replete with game animals. In the center of the valley was the village, with stout huts and communal halls built to withstand the powerful summer storms.

Cala brushed her long black hair to the side and kissed her husband's cheek. "Our children will take pride in your honor. I love you so much." Tears spilled from Cala's dark eyes despite her effort to hold them back. She did not allow her smile to falter. "I know how important it is that someone be a Pollinator. The trees ensure that our island is fruitful. With them, we never know hunger. And the tree dwellers protect us from our enemies. But…" Cala choked and could not continue.

Alika held his wife's face in his brown hands. He marveled at her beauty and kissed her lips. Still she trembled.

"Cala, the trees need a Pollinator. Our family is due to provide the next one. Our two daughters are too young to offer the service. Not that I would have allowed them to while I was still alive."

"Then me…"

"No," Alika said. "After I perform my service, the tribe will provide for you. And the girls will need their mother as they grow and mature."

Cala embraced Alika, though she was careful to not disturb the fragile torc around his neck. "Alika…"

"Go now," Alika fought to keep his own churning emotions under control. He kissed her once more then broke their embrace. "Go to our daughters. Tell them that I love them."

Cala wiped her eyes and nodded. She turned from her husband and walked down the slope. Two young, tear-stained girls awaited her with outstretched arms. Alika looked to the top of the ridge. At the crest was a tree of medium height. Its trunk was twisted and covered with grooved bark. The branches were enfolded in a thick blanket of white strands which filtered the morning sunlight. The web billowed out from a breeze coming off the ocean on the other side of the ridge.

He walked to the top. Once there he looked out over the sand that merged into the blue, endless water. The remains of three war canoes rested on dried clumps of grass. At Alika's feet spears were stacked like driftwood, the wooden shafts gray with exposure to sun and wind. He turned toward the tree. Alika saw another web-enshrouded tree in the distance. The ridge that surrounded the island held hundreds of such trees, all of them spaced evenly apart.

Several gossamer threads broke away from the branches. They floated down and looped around Alika's arms and torso. They were soft but adhered to his flesh, and though they seemed thin and fragile they lifted him effortlessly, as a mother would a child. The web parted and he was brought into the interior of the tree.

Alika was set down upon a thick bough that was warm to the touch. The leaves of the tree were narrow and red, with sharp, serrated edges. Within the web several human bones and skulls hung like ornaments. Loose clusters of blue and white feathers, headdresses of enemy warriors from a neighboring island, hung in tatters from the sticky threads.

A shadow fell upon Alika as a spider, nearly as big as a man, crept down from the upper branches. The spider's coloration, like the tree, was brown and red, and its four pairs of black eyes studied Alika with cold intelligence. One of its furry legs lifted the torc of dead bees from his chest. After a few seconds the torc was laid back down.

The spider lowered its thick abdomen into a cluster of leaves that shielded a green stamen. Gooey strands of web issued out, which the spider's back legs quickly shaped into a funnel that connected the abdomen to the tree's organ.

Curved fangs, translucent and hollow, emerged from the spider's head. Alika watched as they filled with a murky green fluid. Once the fangs were full the spider separated itself from the stamen.

Alika shook as fear took hold of him, but he thought of his wife and daughters, of the needs of the tribe and the entire island. He closed his eyes and arched back his head.

The fangs sank into his throat. Alika's blood burned as the green fluid drained into his body. Mercifully, it did not take long to lose consciousness.

\#

Alika woke to find himself carried by four men from his tribe. His blood was still hot, but the pain was tolerable. He looked at

130

his hand. It was bloated, with the skin stretched taut. His fingernails were green.

He was carried up the slope on another part of the island. They reached the crest and the men, with gentle reverence, lowered him to the ground. In silence they walked back down the slope.

Alika felt himself being lifted.

Inside, the tree was old and diseased.

A spider, identical to the first one, dropped down. It attached its abdomen to a round gourd.

Alika could not stop the tears as they ran in hot rivulets down his face. He kept his family's faces in his thoughts as he offered his neck.

The spider drained Alika of his pollinated blood and fed it into the ovule, which contained a seed. The leaves of the tree caressed the Pollinator's body with gratitude.

#

The sapling was healthy. The spider watched from a distance as humans from the valley chopped down the dead tree and pulled its loose roots from the ground. The tribesmen carried the wood, along with the bones of the Pollinator, down the slope to a waiting fire.

The spider, older than the eldest among the humans, turned and entered the valley forest to wait for its new home to mature.

Saturn Conjunct

Iris brushed back a strand of blonde hair and studied the bi-wheel chart. The inner wheel was Art's natal chart, with all of the planets in their terrible, afflicted glory. The outer wheel was an event chart, based on planetary positions over the town at 10:45 PM, ten minutes from now. Immediately after 10:45 the Moon would exit Virgo and be Void for two and a half hours before it entered Libra. The police response had to happen during this brief window.

She looked out the bay windows at the winter darkness. A long drive, glistening with black ice, snaked through the clusters of trees from the road to her home. Iris wondered how fast Art would drive under these hazardous conditions. Mars was prominent in his First House. Iris smiled. Art would have the accelerator to the floor.

Iris took a sip from the porcelain cup at her elbow. She swished the spicy chai tea around her mouth before she swallowed. Within minutes she knew would see a set of headlights coming fast down the drive. While one did not need to be a slave to the characteristics they were born under, some, like Art, embraced them.

#

"Heather, please reconsider this. You gave me the data to draw up his chart. You've always trusted my advice. Please trust me now. Art is no good. Get rid of him."

Heather shared the same blonde hair and hazel eyes of her

older sister. She folded her arms across her chest and shook her head. "You're wrong this time, Iris. Art's not as bad as you're making him out to be. He's decent and charming. He's never once disagreed with me, let alone raised his voice or, like you have suggested, become in any way violent. He's just not like that."

"Heather, he's charming because he has Mercury in Libra. That will make anyone silver-tongued. But he has Mars in his First House with an Aries Ascendant. If that wasn't bad enough he has Uranus in his Fourth House under affliction and squared against the Ascendant. And he has transiting Pluto conjunct Moon in the Eighth House under Scorpio. Those are aspects of violence and death. To see all of this in a person's natal chart...it's just scary. Art is capable of terrible things, and nowhere in his chart do I see restraint."

Heather turned away. "You're wrong."

"Have I been wrong yet about any of the men in your life? Hasn't each chart I've drawn up for you been an accurate reflection of their characters? Heather, I know you think you really like this guy, but he is all wrong. Please believe me."

Heather looked up, her face set in stone. Iris's heart sank as she saw her sister's Moon in stubborn Taurus come to the fore.

"You're wrong this time, Iris. You wait and see."

#

Two weeks into the relationship Art insisted on moving in with Heather. A week after that Heather got her first shiner. She insisted it was due to her own clumsiness. Iris pointed out that Heather had taken five years of ballet lessons and was one of the least clumsy people in the world. When Heather finally admitted the black eye was given by Art she was quick to insist it was her fault, that she had provoked him. Iris again pleaded with her sister to dump Art. Heather just shook her head.

Heather and Iris could not go out to lunch together without Heather's cell phone ringing every five minutes. Art demanded to know who she was with and when she was coming home. Heather admitted to Iris that Art was always checking her cell phone to see what calls were made, and he was constantly snooping through her e-mail.

#

"I'm calling the police, Heather. I'm sick of seeing this animal treat you like this."

"Iris, no, don't! Please, there's no need for that."

"No need? Heather, fucking wake up! If something isn't done he is going to put you in the ground."

"Jesus Christ, you're blowing it all out of proportion! It's not that bad. Art is right when he says you like to stick your nose in other people's business. Leave it alone, Iris!"

"Listen to yourself, Heather! Listen to the crap you're spewing out. Please, get away from him. Get a restraining order. You can stay with me until he clears out of your place."

"You just don't get it! Leave me alone. Leave us alone."

#

Iris lived at the end of a long drive in a house outside of town. The area was heavily wooded, with venerable yet hardy elm, oak, and maple trees concealing her property from the interstate a quarter-mile away. Her nearest neighbor was Mrs. Venditti, a

134

very pleasant widow who visited once or twice a week to share a cup of tea and chitchat.

When Iris heard the car pull in front of her house she smiled, made sure the tea was ready for Mrs. Venditti, and opened the door.

Art shoved his way in, his tall, powerful body nearly knocking Iris to the floor. He stood and looked at the charts and graphs on Iris's work desk.

"What a load of rubbish," he said. His lips curled in disdain. "I can't believe you're trying to fill Heather's head with all this shit. Who the fuck actually believes in this nowadays?"

"Get out of here!" Iris tried to keep her anger on top of her fear. "You're not welcome in this house. Get out!"

Art turned to her. His dark eyes glittered and his thick, bestial hair stood on end. White, carnivorous teeth flashed in a smile. "Is that any way to treat someone who is practically family? Come on now, Iris, how about some hospitality?"

Iris turned toward the telephone.

Steel fingers gripped her shoulder. "I'd hate to see that phone, or anything else, get damaged. We're not done talking yet."

Iris jerked away from Art's hand. She did not try to move toward the phone. "What do you want?"

"You mean you don't know? What kind of an astrologer are you? I thought you could see into the future."

Iris remained silent. She resisted the urge to rub her bruised shoulder.

Art chuckled. "It's simple, really, what I want. I want you to mind your own fucking business. I want you to stop filling Heather's head with all your shit. In fact, I want you to stop talking to Heather, period. She doesn't want to talk to you or see you anymore, anyway. So keep out of our lives."

Iris glanced toward the telephone.

With a quickness that belied his size Art was upon her. He grabbed her hair and forced her face up to his. His lips mashed against hers and his tongue pushed its way into her mouth like a fat serpent. Iris struggled and tried to scream. Art pulled away before Iris's teeth clamped down.

He backed away and smacked his lips. "Mmmm, you taste just like your sister. I bet you're   livelier in bed, though."

Iris spat on the floor, the taste of Art's tongue thick in her mouth.

Art's face stilled. "Just remember what I said, bitch. You keep the fuck out of our lives. If I have to come back, I won't be nearly as nice."

"Get out! Just get out!"

Art smiled and left. Outside, his fiery red Mustang roared to life and shot down the drive, coming dangerously close to the trees as it flung back loose pebbles.

Iris locked the door and walked to the kitchen. She sat on a wooden stool next to the pot of tea. It took a long time for her to stop shaking.

\#

She should have called the police. She didn't, fearing it would solve nothing and put Heather even more in the line of fire.

Iris would never forgive herself for that decision.

The form in the hospital bed was barely recognizable as her sister. Heather's face was swollen and garish with bruises. Her left cheekbone and orbital socket were shattered. She was unconscious and the doctors weren't sure when she would awaken. They had assured Iris that Heather would recover but that another beating as severe as this could very well result in brain damage or death.

Iris held Heather's cold, unresponsive hand. Tears glittered and spilled out of her eyes.

#

He was out on bail. Un-fucking-believable. The cops had arrested Art, and then the idiotic fucking judge had actually granted the defense lawyer's request and set bail, which Art made. Now the beast was free as a fucking lark until he was sentenced for the aggravated battery charge his douchbag lawyer had plea-bargained for, as it was now clear that Heather would pull through and the prosecution would not have a manslaughter charge. Art would get a year or two in prison at the most.

There was no doubt in Iris's mind that Art would return to Heather once he was out. And Heather, damn her, would take him back.

That was unacceptable.

Iris did a location chart for the town and plotted its progressions until she found what she needed. A Mars/Saturn conjunct, with Mars in retrograde, squaring Art's Ascendant, along with retrograde Mercury in the Third House, and a transiting Uranus in the Eighth House squared against Art's natal Sun. All of which fell in an hour ruled by Saturn, just before a Void Moon.

This astrological event would occur at 10:45 PM in three more nights, the last Friday in January. Iris took the time to redo the chart to ensure that her calculations were correct. There was no variation. It was perfect.

The apartment Art was staying at was about a half-hour from

Iris's house. With the way he drove that made it closer to twenty minutes. And in the mood Art would be in once he was done talking to Iris it would probably take him no more than fifteen minutes.

#

On Friday night Iris swallowed down her nerves and called Art's cell phone. Timing was everything. She dialed at 10:20, certain their conversation would not last long.

After two rings Art answered. "Who's this?"

Art's voice brought Iris's anger to the fore. "It's retribution catching up to you, you piece of shit. It's time for you to pay for what you did to Heather, and I'm not talking about jail time."

"Iris? What the fuck are you talking about?"

"I'm talking about cosmic justice, you cocksucker. You're not going to get off as easy as you think you are."

"Iris, you'd better stop right now if you know what's good for you."

"Fuck you, Art. It's time to flush you down the toilet."

"Iris, shut the fuck up or I'll..."

Iris cut him off. "You'll do nothing, you fucking pussy. I'm not my sister. You can't fuck with me."

"You don't fucking think so, huh?" Art's rage entered the red zone and Iris knew she had him. "You'd better fucking run, bitch, 'cause I'm going to show you just how much I can fuck with you!" The phone clicked off.

10:25. It would take Art a couple of minutes to grab his jacket and jump into his car. Then he would push that red Mustang to its limit over roads that were slippery with ice. But the main roads would have been treated and Art had some skill as a driver, so he would make it to Iris's drive. It was essential that he reach her drive.

The minutes crept by. Each one tore a little more from her nerves. Iris could sense the planets above moving along their assigned, inalterable paths. The planets did not care about what was happening below. Their business transcended anything that puny humans could devise. 10:35 turned into 10:40. Iris took a sip of her chai tea and willed herself to calm down, telling herself that everything was happening as it should. She looked at her watch. 10:44.

What if he wasn't coming? What if Art got held up in traffic, or was pulled over for speeding?

That would ruin everything. Then she would need to run.

Headlights stabbed through the trees, twisting at the drive's serpentine angles and approaching at a fast rate of speed.

Iris took a deep, steadying breath and looked at her watch. 10:45.

A moment of perfect conjunct between Saturn and a retrograde Mars, with a retrograde Mercury in the Third House, which produced poor judgment and mechanical failure, especially if affecting those whose natal chart showed considerable affliction. Like Art's.

A fuel line blockage caused the Mustang to stall and lose its power steering just as its wide tires hit a patch of black ice. The tires clawed for traction that was not there and could not swerve from a massive elm tree. The muscle car plowed into the trunk with an explosion of screeching metal and glittering, fragmented glass.

Iris rushed to the door and cracked it open, listening for any movement. Remarkably, the Mustang's headlights still illuminated the area, though the angles of the lights were skewed in unnatural directions. There was a slight hissing sound.

Iris put on her coat and grabbed a long kitchen knife. She walked the fifty or so yards in the cold darkness toward the wreck. The hissing sound came from a radiator that had been shorn in half. The hood of the car was buckled into a "U" shape around the gouged trunk of the tree. Sections of the engine rested in the front seat.

Art lay face-down in the drive on a bed of pebbled glass that shone like bloody diamonds.

He hadn't been wearing a seat belt. Upon impact Art had flown through the windshield.

His body was torn, broken, and still.

Iris checked her watch. 10:55. The planets above continued on their courses, unconcerned with the tiny piece of carnage beneath them.

The Moon was leaving Virgo. In two and a half hours it would enter Libra. During those two and a half hours the Moon would be Void, a time when a lot of commonplace things got messed up. Details, routinely handled, were missed. Like those from an accident scene investigation.

The police response would take about ten minutes. They would request an ambulance, even though it was obvious the driver was beyond medical help. They would question Iris, but they knew who Art was. They would assume that Art had a grudge against his girlfriend's sister and was looking to settle matters before going to prison. Iris would express shock and surprise. And the Void Moon would keep the police from seeing Iris's number as the last call received on Art's cell phone.

Iris walked back to her home and dialed 911. "Hello? I'd like to report an accident..."

A Face for Every Need

The old man opened the doors on the wall-mounted steel cabinet.

Steffan was shocked at how many keys there were. There were thousands of them, all individually numbered.

"So many to choose from," he said. "How can I possibly know which one I need?"

The old man was bald, with liver spots covering his parchment-like skin. His thin form was stooped, and his hands curled into claws. Despite his age, the blue eyes deep within the wrinkles of his face were clear and alert.

"You filled the form out honestly?" the old man asked.

"Yes," Steffan nodded.

"Then I have an idea as to what you need." The old man turned to the open cabinet and took away three keys from those numbered in the four hundreds.

"This way."

The old man led Steffan through a door into an empty room. Recessed safes covered the walls, each about a foot square, all individually numbered with their own keyholes. It was obvious each one corresponded with one of the keys in the other room.

The old man shuffled up to the four hundreds. He took a key and inserted it into the keyhole of safe 401. He turned the key and the door opened.

Inside was a plastic, featureless head covered with a skin-like mask with holes for the eyes, nostrils, and mouth. The old man peeled the mask away from the plastic mount and held it out to Steffan.

"Try this one."

As Steffan took it he suppressed a cringe. It felt like real human skin. But it was elastic enough for him to pull down over his own head.

The material fit the contours of his cranium and adhered to the planes of his face perfectly. Steffan stared at the old man through the eye holes.

"Now what?" he asked.

"Give it a second," the old man said.

The inner lining of the mask seeped into the pores of Steffan's skin and anchored itself in place. He gasped and tried to remove it…

Nothing was ever given to me. Everything I have, I earned. It was my ideas and my determination that made me the man I am today. So I'll be damned if I allow one little bookkeeper to take it all away. I've always let him shave a little off the top. I wouldn't have trusted him otherwise. But now he wants to be a partner. And he's threatening to turn me in to the IRS if I don't make him one. Okay, let him think he has me over a barrel. We'll celebrate his newfound "promotion" at Gillespie's, and while we're eating, the Bowvan brothers will sneak into his car. When the bookkeeper leaves to go home, flush with his imagined victory, he'll be taken for a ride from which he'll never return.

The mask pulled away from Steffan's face. He drew in a ragged breath.

The old man chuckled. "It takes you by surprise at first, doesn't it?"

Steffan ripped the mask from his head.

"Easy with that," the old man chided. He smoothed it out and put it back on its plastic base. "Are you sure you want to continue?"

Despite the shock of the experience, Steffan knew he couldn't walk away. He had paid too much money. "Yes."

"Very well." The old man unlocked the next door with key 412. The safe contained another plastic head and skin mask. He pulled off the mask and gave it to Steffan, who after a moment's hesitation put it on. The lining melded with his face almost immediately.

Out of all my dealers, I never expected Jimmie to be the one to rat on me. If I hadn't seen him talking to the narc with my own eyes I never would have believed it. But there it was. Motherfucker. I need to make an example of him. A bullet to the brain isn't enough. I need to make my other dealers more afraid of me than they are of the narcs. Jimmie needs to suffer. The fact that he's my cousin will really drive it home to the rest.

The mask pulled away.

Steffan took it off, more gently this time. "Can I try one more?"

The old man nodded and took the mask from him. He unlocked the last door, labeled 420, and handed the mask to Steffan.

When the mask adhered to him, Steffan was shocked to find he was now a woman.

That promotion was mine. I put in all the hours and the work. I sacrificed everything, including my marriage, for this goal. And now she jumps in and takes all of the credit. And the company believes her! They're giving her the promotion, the corner office, and the salary! No! Not on my watch, bitch. We're both going on that business trip to Arizona. There are a lot of isolated spaces for you to have an "accident".

Steffan took the mask off and the old man put it away. "Do either of these masks suit you, or do you want to try more?"

143

Steffan had already decided. "I'll take the first one."

The old man nodded and retrieved the first mask. Steffan slipped it on.

"Would you like a mirror?" the old man asked.

"Yes."

Steffan was led to a wall mirror that hung between two rows of safes. His short red hair was now slicked back and gray. The shape of his face had changed, from a round forty-year-old's to the thin, acerbic face of someone twenty-five years older. His brown eyes were now a blazing green.

Steffan smiled with lips that were not his. "Perfect."

Not Your Grandfather's Hades

Hi! My name is Doug, and I'll be ferrying you across the Styx. Charon? Oh, he retired two centuries ago. He put in his five thousand years with the FIC... Federation of Infernal Creatures, Local 216. Charon is collecting a very good pension. He has a place on the banks of the Phlegethon. He catches a chill easy, and the boiling blood of the Phlegethon help to keep him warm.

The skiff will accommodate everyone. Please, watch your step. And no pushing. We can't have anyone falling in the water. It's very cold and, quite frankly, I don't appreciate the lost time it takes for me to fish someone out. I may just leave you there. Just like that guy. See him, trying to climb in the skiff? Well, this pole of mine isn't just for pushing the boat from one bank to the other. There! Even though he's just a shade, he felt that. And there he goes, tumbling away downstream. Maybe someday I'll allow him to climb in. Maybe.

Is everybody in? Okay, here we go. I advise everybody to not look over the side. That guy I knocked away? He's not the only one in the Styx. And as new shades, none of you are as yet equipped to resist the pull of more experienced shades. If you make eye contact with someone in there, most likely you'll be joining them.

Oh, thank you, ma'am! But you don't have to pay me for transport. We get funding from taxes collected by the Underworld Board. What's that, sir? Oh, yes, I'm afraid so. Just because you're dead, that doesn't mean you stop paying taxes. Now, now, no need to wail! Everyone pays as they can. This will all be explained to you by Placement representatives once you reach the far bank. The fat cats in Elysium are given some pretty decent tax breaks. But you didn't hear that from me.

Yes, ma'am, Placement reps. Minos was cashiered out a long time ago. Yes, it's too bad. He didn't want to go, but he was getting slow and sloppy, so the Underworld Board did the math and realized that a trained team of Placement reps would not only do a quicker and more accurate job in placements, they would be cheaper, as well. Minos filed a grievance, but a bylaw established in the last collective bargaining agreement five hundred years ago stated that his position was a lead position, eligible to be elevated to a supervisory position at the Board's discretion. So they elevated him to a supervisor, effectively taking him out of the Union. Once that happened, he was made to resign. He's getting a full supervisor's pension, but he's still very unhappy about it.

I don't know where you'll end up, sir. Chances are you will go to the Asphodel Meadows. It's not nearly as swanky as Elysium, but it's still nice. There's a lot of development going on there. New condos go up all the time. Malls are being developed, and hellhounds are available for adoption at the local kennel. Once you go through the orientation and have been given quarters to stay, you will all take aptitude tests to see what jobs you'll be given. What's that, sir? You're retired? Well, you were retired from your job in the living world. That doesn't count down here. Please, sir, don't take it so hard. I think you'll like the job you're given. In fact, I'm certain that whatever jobs you chose to do in life will be mirrored in the Underworld.

More wailing? Come on, people, it's not that bad. It'll be worse for those of you who will end up in Tartarus. It's very dark in Tartarus. There's no running water or electricity. You'll be made to live in a filthy apartment infested with imps. And

146

you'll be assigned a social worker, who will push you into horrible, low-paying jobs, like cleaning the latrines of the demons. Drug-addicted ghouls sprawl on every street corner, and succubi will tempt you into giving them your essence, until there is nothing left. Gangs of vicious cambions roam everywhere, giving savage beatings to shades wherever they go. Worst of all are the bill collectors. I can't even talk about them.

So now you see that the Asphodel Meadows aren't so bad, after all. And after a century of work, you'll have an opportunity to join your own union, the Association of Collective Shades. When that happens, in addition to paying taxes, you'll be paying union dues, as well.

Elysium? Well, I don't want to say there is *no* chance, but… we need to be realistic. Only certain individuals are allowed into Elysium. Members are voted on while they are still alive by the Elysium Upper Echelon. Yes, that means it's invitation only. Well, yes, sir, there have been occasions when someone from the Asphodel Meadows has done exceptionally well in their chosen field and been noticed by the EUE, but that is very seldom. Those in Elysium prefer their own kind.

Okay, here we are, everybody. Please disembark in an orderly manner. And as you make your way to the gate, remember one last thing. Do *not* pet the dog, even if he has three heads. Cerberus doesn't like that. He'll rip your arm off if you try. It's painful, and it takes a long time to reform another arm.

Enjoy your stay!

Red Cup

The seed's shell cracked. A shoot pushed up through the soil, striving for the surface and sunlight. It broke through into the brightness of a new life as its roots dove into the ground, absorbing life-giving nutrients and water.

The plant continued to grow through many cycles of sunlight, rain, and darkness. Its stem extended beyond the grass that surrounded it. A bud sprouted at the end. After a few days, with help from a warm, caressing sun, the bud opened. Orange and black petals blossomed from a deep red center.

The plant named itself Red Cup.

Red Cup thrived with the other plants that grew around it. They chatted back and forth, and soaked in cool water when it rained.

Then one day Red Cup found that it could pull its roots from the ground and move from place to place.

The other plants did not like that.

#

Red Cup bloomed with the coming of the morning sun. A slender stamen, quivering with pollen, protruded from the red center.

Red Cup pulled his roots from the soft earth. He cast about, looking for willing pistils, or at least a bee to deliver the pollen for him. Even a good gust of wind would do.

He pulled himself forward with his roots, drinking in surface dew as he went. Grass, proud and obstinate, tried to block his way. *What makes you so special?* Each blade turned and hissed at Red Cup. *You think you're better than us because you can move from place to place?*

Red Cup did not answer the taunts as he crept forward. He never did.

He zigzagged around the crabgrass. Crabgrass was meaner and much stronger than regular grass.

Something big slapped Red Cup in the petals and nearly knocked him over. He turned and with dismay noticed he had stumbled into a patch of dandelions. This was bad.

A big yellow flower got right into Red Cup's petals. *And where do you think you're going?* The dandelion's sharp petals pushed at his stamen. Pollen trickled uselessly to the ground. *You think you're going to find a home for that? Think again, freak.*

Red Cup was shoved from behind by the thick, serrated leaf of another dandelion. *We're going to knock that pollen right off of you. You're not contaminating anything, walker.*

Blows fell on Red Cup from every direction. He searched desperately for an opening with which to escape. Dark leaves blocked him. The ground about him was coated with red pollen dust. Red Cup tried to fold his petals together to protect the stamen, but the dandelions held them open.

A low susurration vibrated through the early morning air. The dandelions paused in their pummeling of Red Cup. The sound intensified, becoming a buzzing that engulfed their senses. The yellow heads of the dandelions swiveled up in anticipation.

A bumblebee, its huge body covered in black and yellow fur, hovered overhead.

The small yellow petals of the dandelions parted to reveal twin curlicue stamens. *Me! Me! My nectar is sweet! Take my pollen!*

They all shouted up at the bee, who flew tantalizingly from one flower to the next without landing on any.

They had forgotten about Red Cup. He moved his roots carefully around the dandelion stems and pulled himself away from their grasp.

Red Cup wandered around a patch of clovers. Clovers were generally self-absorbed and did not bother with other plants, but Red Cup knew from experience that if he mingled with them, they would try to hold him in place. Red Cup was stronger than any individual clover, but it was tough to slog out of a middle of a patch.

Red Cup turned to the sky. The sun was more than halfway across. He looked around for bees or butterflies. A few buzzed or fluttered, but none came near him. It seemed even insects sensed he was different and avoided him.

Ahead was a large rock that bordered a vegetable garden. If Red Cup could pull himself upon it, maybe a good gust of wind would take his remaining pollen and blow it to a few exposed stigmas.

Something hit the ground.

Red Cup froze. He pushed a root into the earth and waited. A steady *thump-THUMP* came closer.

Oh, no…

Red Cup pushed his roots into the ground as far as they could go. He folded his petals over his stamen. He curled his stem and tried to hide his colors.

A rabbit looked about, twitching its nose. Black eyes in a brown-furred face found Red Cup.

The rabbit hopped toward him.

Red Cup clutched the earth as hard as he could. The rabbit sniffed his petals. Red Cup heard the other plants laughing and urging the rabbit on.

The rabbit chewed on Red Cup's petals. Severed pieces fell to the earth. The rabbit nibbled away at the stamen and worked its way down. Red Cup was frozen in agony. He screamed as his stem was ripped from his roots by one of the rabbit's paws. The surrounding grass shrieked with delight.

The rabbit bit deep into his dark red center, hungry for nectar. It squealed and backed away, spitting out what it had bitten off. Red Cup did not understand. Was the rabbit rejecting him, like the plants and bees did?

Red Cup's consciousness bled away from his torn and mangled flower and collected back into his roots.

The rabbit hopped away as Red Cup's thoughts faded into nothingness.

#

His world was pain and struggle. All was dark as Red Cup's roots strove to heal. He willed himself to grow again. He couldn't lose his focus on that one task. To do so would be death.

Red Cup pushed against the earth above him. It did not yield. Red Cup wanted to give up. *No. No, I can't.* He sucked in more nutrients from the soil and pushed harder.

The ground gave way. Early morning sunlight bathed Red Cup's new shoot as it pushed upward, his chlorophyll soaking in the light and using its energy to grow ever further.

Several days passed as Red Cup grew stronger. His stem elongated and sprouted a bud. The grass whispered invectives at

151

him, but he did not listen. He needed to concentrate on blossoming.

As he matured, Red Cup thought about his existence. How had he come into being? Who was responsible for fertilizing his seed, allowing him to germinate and live? There were no other plants like him around. How was it he was able to move around, while other plants couldn't?

No answers came. Red Cup resigned himself to the fact that they probably never would.

The humidity in the air was thick when Red Cup's petals finally opened to the sun. Black and orange colors spread wide to reveal a long red pistil, sprouting from an ovule-rich ovary. At its tip, a stigma, round and sticky, tested the air.

Immediately the grass passed the word to the other plants. *Watch where your pollen goes! Make sure it's nowhere near the freak!*

Red Cup pulled her roots from the ground. She looked for the rock she had seen before and started toward it. If she could climb it and elevate herself above the other pistils, there was a good chance a bee would land on her and give her pollen.

The grass was taller and thicker than she remembered. Red Cup still pushed through it, but it was more of a struggle. The sheer number of green blades tripped her up more than once. Red Cup did her best to ignore the snarling hatred around her.

A low hum moved through the air. The grass blades stilled; waves of dread ran through them. Red Cup knew what the sound was, and she hurried around stalks which now ignored her.

The hum turned into a roar that reverberated through the ground. Grass, dandelions, clovers, foxtails, sorrels, all screamed. Red Cup willed her roots to move faster.

The rock lay just ahead. The roar turned into an all-encompassing blast that quickly bore down on her.

Red Cup was not going to make it.

She saw the horror approaching. Red Cup folded her petals around her pistil and bent her stem as low as she could. Her roots sought quick purchase in the ground. She hoped it would be enough.

Darkness engulfed Red Cup, and a terrible wind buffeted her. Just above her, a thick, slicing maelstrom tore into the grass. Juice and dismembered bits of green bounced off her.

Just as quickly as the darkness came, it was gone.

The grass cried and moaned. Their tops had been sliced off. Juice and plant bits lay everywhere. Red Cup glanced up at the uncaring, towering human who pushed the cruel machine as it continued to rip through the greenery. She stayed low. If the human saw her standing upright, he would come back with the machine until she shared the same fate as those around her.

Next to Red Cup was the severed head of a dandelion. The ragged stem bled green. Red Cup wondered if it was one of her tormentors, and then decided it didn't matter. A flower's life was in the roots, not the head. The dandelion whose head this was would grow another. And probably still be a bully.

The awful roaring of the machine sputtered and stopped. The human wheeled it away. The grass was in shock and pain, and Red Cup pushed through with no resistance.

The rock lay a few feet away.

The grass blades stirred as Red Cup made her careful way between them. One that the machine had missed took a swipe at her, but was not strong enough to delay her progress.

The rock was right in front of her.

A number of small purple flowers peeked up from where they had been hiding at the base of the rock. They looked around to make sure the human was gone.

Henbits. If they saw Red Cup, they would never let her climb on the rock. They had broad, strong leaves that would stop her cold.

But they were distracted. Red Cup might have a chance.

Red Cup crept forward as fast as she could. She extended a root over the purple head of one of the henbits and touched the rock. She anchored the root in a small crevice.

The purple flower spun around as Red Cup reached out with two more roots. Wide, crenellated leaves lifted up to stop them. *What do you think you're doing, walker? This rock is off-limits to you.* The henbit called out to the others. *Help me rip this freak's roots off and kill it before it has a chance to germinate any seeds!*

Red Cup pushed against the henbit's leaves. Her second root found purchase on the rough surface of the rock. The third grasped a tiny outcrop but was torn away by the henbit.

The other henbits within reach pushed at Red Cup's stem. One tried to dislodge the two roots she had secured to the rock. Red Cup stretched again with the third root. It slid across the hard surface without finding purchase. It was knocked away.

The henbit resistance was now coordinated. Leaves with serrated edges scraped across Red Cup's stem. Fluid leaked from small gashes.

Red Cup weakened. One of her two roots was plucked free from the rock. She struggled to reattach it.

The last root was pulled away. Red Cup was thrown to the ground.

The henbits continued to attack, tearing at Red Cup until she dragged herself out of their reach.

Next time you try that, we'll kill you, walker! We'll tear your roots apart! Do us all a favor and go off and die! There's no place for you here!

Red Cup made her way to a mercifully bare patch of soil. The surrounding grass was still stunned from the human's machine and did not try to hinder her. She looked up and noticed she was in the shade of a young poplar. The tree ignored her. Most trees couldn't be bothered with smaller plants, conversing only with fellow hardwoods. Even a plant that could walk was below their notice. Red Cup had never been more thankful. She sank her roots into the ground to absorb what she needed to heal.

Hey.

Red Cup raised her flower. A plant she had never seen before, thick with oval-shaped leaves, grew at the base of the tree.

Red Cup lay back down. Whatever the plant was, it couldn't reach her. Let it spew its hatred at her. She would not answer.

I know what you are. I've seen your kind before.

Despite herself, Red Cup turned to the plant. *Who are you?*

I am a chipilin, the plant said. *I am not native to this area. I come from a place far to the south. As do you. You are a bane orchid. There aren't many of you.*

Red Cup stood and approached the chipilin. *If we are not native to this place, then why are we here?*

We were brought over unwittingly by the humans. I was a young plant that somehow got mixed with a crate of mangoes. Once I got here the crate was broken up and discarded, along with me. I would have died had not a rainstorm washed me down several roads and into this yard. That was many, many seasons ago. The winters here are not to my liking, but they are not cold enough to kill me. I hope I can say the same for you.

I don't remember coming here.

The chipilin rustled its leaves. *You probably came over as a seed, possibly mixed up with a crate of fruit as well. Either way, here we are.*

Red Cup heard a strange buzzing noise in the distance. *The other plants hate me. They tear out my roots when they can and stop me from pollinating. You are the only one who hasn't tried to kill me.*

That's because you are able to move around. Plus, you are able to change genders with each new flowering. Some plants have both genders, but very few can change as quickly as you. Those are huge advantages for a plant, and they are jealous of it.

I can't help that! It's just who I am.

It doesn't matter. You are different, and you have abilities they yearn for and will never get. They will never stop hating you.

Red Cup shook her petals. *So I am doomed. The other plants will find a way to tear me from the ground and prevent me from rooting. I will die, and they will be happy.*

The buzzing sound grew in intensity.

The chipilin did its best to flatten out its leaves on the ground. *Get down. Now.*

Red Cup did not need more persuasion. A shock of fear ran through her as she realized what the buzzing was.

The same human as before stepped into view, this time holding something that looked like a huge, inverted flower. The roots, which were held up, appeared to be bundled into a knot at one end of a long, thick stem, while the head, with one large petal and two thin stamens, swooped low to the ground. The human pressed a leaf on the stem. The new machine that looked like a flower roared. The stamens spun with shocking violence, churning up stray plants that the first machine had missed.

The human approached the rock that Red Cup had tried to climb. The henbits that guarded it screamed as the spinning stamens tore through them. Purple petals and minced bits of leaf scattered everywhere. Red Cup shivered as pieces fell near her.

The terrible noise subsided and the human moved on.

Red Cup did not move until the chipilin told her it was safe to do so.

She turned toward the rock. Green juice dripped from its surface. At its base, the severed stems of the henbits were stilled.

If Red Cup had succeeded in climbing the rock…

The henbits, though they didn't mean to, had saved Red Cup's life. Her roots, on the rock and not anchored in the ground, would have withered and died after her stem had been severed by one of the spinning stamens.

Red Cup felt she should be horrified by what happened to the henbits. She wasn't. The henbits and all the other plants would have been happy to see the same happen to her.

Only one thing concerned Red Cup now. She turned to the chipilin. *How far south must I go to find my own kind?*

I'm not sure, the chipilin said. *But, judging by the angle of the sun during the seasons, I sense the distance is great.*

Red Cup considered this. *I cannot remain here. I must go.*

I understand. The journey will be long and hazardous, but at least you have a weapon at your disposal to deal with hostile plants and herbivores.

What weapon?

Are you not aware that you are an allelopathic plant?

Red Cup stood still. Something about that word sent a shiver through her. *What does that mean?*

The chipilin chuckled. *Of course. Foolish of me not to realize you wouldn't know. You would have found out about it through your kin. But you have no kin here.*

Her leaves fluttering with impatience, Red Cup asked again. *Please, tell me. What does allelopathic mean?*

It means you have a store of chemicals, deep in the heart of your flower, that can be used to drive away herbivorous animals.

Red Cup remembered the rabbit, and its reaction when it had bitten into her flower's center.

The chipilin continued. *And can also be used to kill other plants.*

This caught Red Cup's attention. *How do I use these chemicals?*

The chipilin paused, as if carefully considering its answer. *Focus on the depths of your flower. There should be a little knot there, made up of small petals. Do you feel it?*

Red Cup sensed the knot. Now that she was focused on it, she realized there was something within the petals, something hot and eager for release.

The petals may take some effort to open at first, since you have never done it before. You should practice, before you face real threats out there.

Red Cup looked around. She saw a blade of grass that had been missed by the human's machines and made her way to it.

The blade turned to her. *What do you want, freak?*

Red Cup opened her outer petals as wide as they would go. She concentrated on the smaller ones at the red center of her flower. There were five of them. One quivered and opened. Once that happened, the others quickly followed.

Leaning forward, Red Cup belched the heat onto the grass stem. The fluid was thin and pink, with dark red motes floating within. It oozed into the earth.

What did you do to me, freak? What is...

The grass blade could not stop the osmosis. The roots absorbed the fluid, which collected in the xylem and quickly shot it through the plant's vascular system.

The grass blade lost its voice and shuddered. Its edges and tip turned brown.

Red Cup watched the blade die. A pleasurable shiver ran through her. She looked across the lawn, at all the other plants still reeling from the human's machines, and wished she had enough chemicals to kill them all.

It became clear what Red Cup had to do.

She turned to the chipilin. *You have been kind to me, and taught me about myself. When the time comes, you will be spared.*

The chipilin was quiet a moment. *What are your intentions?*

I am going home, Red Cup said. It was after noon, so she positioned the sun at her right side and pulled herself forward. *It may take many seasons, but I will make it. I will find my own kind. We will multiply.*

Red Cup turned and faced the lawn. *Then I will return. With as many of my kindred as will come with me. Except for you, we will kill all that grows here.*

The humans will not allow that, the chipilin said. *They will kill you on sight.*

The humans will not know we are here. We will spread our chemicals at night, and move off to a hiding spot during the day.

The grass, the dandelions, the henbits…all will die. None will call me a freak again.

Red Cup was now distant from the chipilin, almost out of communication range. *Then we will find a patch of fertile ground, away from human eyes, where we can grow and pollinate. We will expand, and any native plants that try to stop us will be destroyed. By the time the humans realize what we are, we'll be everywhere.*

The chipilin's words were faint. *Good luck.*

Red Cup continued her southward crawl.

An Accidental Damnation

"Your 1:00 is here, sir."

"Thank you, Jezebel," Satan hung up the phone. He groaned and acrid smoke curled from his nostrils. What did the Old Man want now?

The office door opened and an angel entered, all ten feet of him, with a glittering robe and impossibly white wings. Satan folded back his own black, leathery wings. He remembered when he had wings that were even more impressive than those of his visitor. But the price for keeping them had been too much to bear.

Satan indicated a seat on the other side of the desk and the angel sat. He nodded at the green-skinned succubus who had shown the visitor in. "Thank you, Jezebel."

Jezebel looked fearfully at the angel and closed the door quickly behind her.

Satan rested his clawed hands on his charred-wood desk and leaned forward. "What is it, Gabriel? What does the Old Man want?"

Gabriel beatific smile irritated Satan. "Is that a way to greet a former brother? Not even an offer of coffee or tea?"

"You wouldn't like our brand. We brew it with the blood of cherubs. Now cut the crap. Why are you here?"

Gabriel chuckled. "You always were direct. Okay, down to business. The Old Man wants someone you have. Name of Melvin Krombs. He died on earth two days ago."

Satan turned to his computer and clicked a few keys. He found the file and read it, and then looked at Gabriel in bemusement.

"This guy? Are you kidding? He was a hopeless drunkard in life. Do you know how he died? He drank a bottle of nail polish remover. Roll that around on your tongue a few times. *Nail polish remover.* I could claim this as a suicide if Krombs weren't so abysmally stupid."

Gabriel nodded. "I agree, Krombs was an idiot. But he gave his last five dollars to a homeless child. With no money to buy booze, he drank nail polish remover he had found in someone's trash. But, the previous act of generosity caught the Old Man's attention and earned Krombs his absolution. Unfortunately, he drank the remover and died before the paperwork could be processed. However, stupidity is not a sin, and the Old Man wants him."

Satan smiled and wagged a finger. "That's not my problem. Melvin Krombs committed enough sins during life to end up here." He tapped the computer screen with a talon. "I received no absolution from upstairs. And once a soul passes through my gates, that's it. He's mine. The Old Man didn't move fast enough. Too bad."

Gabriel sighed and stood from the chair. His impressive wings fluttered behind him as he took out his cell phone and speed-dialed a long established number.

"Hi Boss... yeah, he's being stubborn. You called it. But I wanted to try first. Yeah... I guess giving the benefit of a doubt doesn't work down here. Do I have your permission to proceed with Plan B? Okay, thanks."

Gabriel disconnected the call.

Satan sat back in satisfaction. "What's Plan B? Going back to the Old Man with nothing but your celestial dick in your hands?"

"Not quite. The humans have a phrase, 'good cop, bad cop'. When the good cop is unable to get the job done, the bad cop is sent in. I, the good cop, couldn't convince you to release Melvin Krombs. So perhaps…"

Gabriel's fair, beautiful features shifted and twisted, becoming dark and angular. His soft body hardened into muscles, and his glittering white gown transformed into brilliant armor. The feathers of his white wings bled until they became a dark crimson. A long, blazing sword materialized in his hand.

"…you need a touch of the bad cop to show you the error of your ways," Michael finished for Gabriel, in a voice that boomed and echoed and blew out one of Satan's office windows, allowing in a sulfurous brimstone breeze.

Jezebel peeked in sheepishly. "Is everything all right?"

Michael swung his sword. Jezebel's head popped off her body and rolled to the corner. The headless body fell to its hands and knees and searched for the missing head, which tried to shout directions from its resting spot a few feet away.

Satan shook his head in exasperation. "Really, Michael? Why do you have to be so melodramatic?"

The point of the flaming sword found Satan's neck. "Melvin Krombs. Now."

Jezebel's hands finally found her head and stuck it back in place. She looked uncertainly to her boss for instruction.

Satan sighed. "You want to bring Krombs back to the Old Man, Michael? Fine, he's yours. If you want, you can take all of the idiots here. Empty this place out, why don't you?"

"I only want Krombs," Michael intoned. Satan reflected that Michael and the Old Man were the only ones who *intoned* when they spoke. Talk about hero worship. "Where is he? I'll get him."

"Oh, no you don't. Hell has been harrowed once already. I don't need for you to do it again." Satan glanced at his receptionist. "Jezebel, I believe Melvin Krombs is in Belial's area. Have Belial bring him up."

"Right away, sir." Jezebel fled the office.

The point of the sword was removed from his neck. Satan realized he would have to spend several uncomfortable minutes alone with the archangel until Krombs was retrieved.

"Now that you're getting what you want, any chance of Gabriel coming back? I can have an actual conversation with him."

Michael stood in silence, his only response a frown.

Fine. So be it. Satan gestured to the broken window. "Once you bring your precious Krombs back, tell the Old Man I want to be reimbursed for that."

Michael glanced at the shattered glass. "Send a requisition. You know the procedure."

Satan shook his head in disgust.

Only in Hell.

A Market for Mortality

Death had just walked into my office.

There was no doubt in my mind as to the identity of my unannounced visitor. The towering figure draped entirely in black, the deep hood that gave only a vague clue of the gleaming skull it contained, the unnerving silence of its movements, and, of course, the trademark scythe held in a firm, skeletal hand.

Death is an arrogant, self-assured son of a bitch. He drifted over to the chair before my desk and seated himself without even a perfunctory "hello". As it was getting late on a Friday afternoon, Death was really beginning to piss me off.

He just sat there, calmly eye-socketing me. A clean skull does not give much away in the form of facial gestures. He nonchalantly draped his scythe across his cloaked knees. I noticed the air had gotten a bit chillier, and this only added to my annoyance. It looked like the ball was in my court.

I asked the first question that came to mind. "How did you get past my receptionist?"

The hood seemed to droop a bit, then it straightened up. "I took her," he managed to rasp without vocal cords, exhaling foul air without, I presumed, lungs.

"You 'took her'? Just what the hell do you mean by that?"

"What part of 'I took her' didn't you understand?" came back Death's surprisingly sarcastic reply. Sarcasm denoted a sense of humor, which I never would have suspected Death of having. "When I 'take' someone, what does that usually mean?"

"Don't get smart-assed with me," I started to retort, then, "You killed her?"

Death shook his cowled head in an exasperated way. "That is

a crude and uneducated way of putting it, but yes, I suppose when you get right down to it, I 'killed' her. I've got her soul right here." Death held up a dark mass that seemed to have a life of its own. It was not that big, just slightly more so than the paper bag that had contained my pastrami on rye. The entire existence of the being that had been my receptionist was that?

"Dolores?" I called out to the amorphous, undulating mass. Amazingly, the thing seemed to hear me. Its movements stopped as if in recognition of the name. "Dolores, what happened?" I implored the seemingly sentient object.

"Oh, for the love of what you call God," Death griped, hiding the… *soul*… in a deft movement. "She can't answer you. She's dead! I made her brain hemorrhage just before she was to call you to tell you she was leaving for the day. It was no big deal. She would have only gotten in the way of the business we have to conduct."

Just who the fuck did Death think he was? Did he have any idea how long it would take to find and properly train a new receptionist? Months! This asshole had just screwed up my whole schedule until June. And now he wanted to talk business?

"Just what kind of 'business' did you have in mind?" I cautiously inquired.

"You are Carlton Edmund Cooper, one of the partners in the advertising firm called The Huntington Group?"

"Did the name plaque on my door give me away?" Anger still burned in me as I strove to prove to Death that I could be as sarcastic as he.

"Cut the shit, Cooper. I'm not some flunkie you can dismiss out-of-hand."

To prove his point, Death raised one of his fleshless hands and pointed a thin white finger at me. My chest began to constrict. I struggled to take in a breath. Sweat broke out of every pore. The pain intensified. My vision blackened, and what little air was in my lungs was expelled as I collapsed across the desk. Suddenly, the pain disappeared, and I was looking down at my own body, watching as a nerve spasm made my right hand knock over a container of pens. Then I saw Death's huge form come up to meet me, a skeletal hand grabbing, ripping, forcing me to his dark bosom, as I struggled, helpless and terrified as a newborn who is thrust unwillingly into a hard, apathetic world.

"Nooooooo!"

Wham! Back in my body, just like that. I sat up and gave myself a quick check-over. No more chest pain. No more labored breathing. The residue of death-sweat stuck to my clothes like cobwebs in an empty corner. But I was still alive.

I looked over at Death, who even without a muscle on his face still managed to smirk. Shaken, I nodded my head. Point taken.

"So," I began, struggling to get my voice under control, the late hour and my plans for the evening forgotten. "Mr., ah, Reaper. Is it all right to call you that?"

Death waved that potent hand of his dismissively.

"Well, then, Mr. Reaper, just what kind of 'business' did you have in mind?"

Death showed true interest for the first time. "I want you and this organization to market me. Positively."

Well. Wasn't this an interesting turn of events? I was being given the exclusive opportunity of marketing Death. But...

"Aren't you already... *popular*... after a certain fashion? It seems that every rock song mentions you at least seven or eight times, not to mention the boost in ratings TV news gets whenever they depict your... more creative activities."

"That's exactly what I'm talking about!" Death exclaimed, actually becoming animated. "That's the image I want to eradicate. The general public is fascinated with me, but for all the wrong reasons. I'm seen as bad, evil, something to dread the inevitable coming of. There's no reason for that way of thinking. All I am is the natural conclusion to this particular phase of existence. In a way, death is just a variation of birth, and nobody fears birth. It's all just a part of the Order."

Wow. This meeting was starting to blow me away. Death made a good argument for himself, but I knew that that alone wouldn't do it. Thousands of years of inbred fear wouldn't instantly vanish after hearing a few eloquent lines. But it was a start. Images were hard to change, especially in this particular case, but it wasn't impossible.

"I think the biggest problem," I began, "isn't you yourself. I think everybody knows you come for them eventually, and deep down, they're resigned to this fact. It seems to me that what they fear most is the *form* in which you'll arrive. Like I indicated before, you can be very creative, and a lot of that creativity has a tendency to cause a lot of physical pain before the individual actually expires. Emotional pain, too, if you come in the form of a prolonged illness. Another big fear is the *time* in a person's life that you arrive for them. Nobody wants to die young, except, of course, for those misguided few who actually force you to come to them when they commit suicide."

"I know," Death replied, the skull inside the cowl actually grimacing. "The notion of suicide has been romanticized for much too long. That idiot Shakespeare really did it with his foolish play *Romeo and Juliet*, especially among teenagers. Asshole!"

Death continued to amaze me. Death cared!

"As to what you call my 'creativity'," Death continued, "that, also, is all part of the natural Order. Pain and suffering is among you for a reason, a good reason. Unfortunately, I cannot divulge that reason, as I cannot divulge what happens to you after I come for you. All I can say is that it's all part of a spirit's 'education'.

"Many among you *think* they know," Death smirked. "But they don't"

I was intrigued. "You mean to say that all the world's religions have it wrong?"

"Yes and no. They all have a piece of the puzzle, but none of them are close to having the full picture. The same is true for those you consider to be 'philosophers'. The ironic part is, each member of the human race, from the moment of birth, already *knows* these 'secrets' that I told you I couldn't divulge. You could learn them for yourself… if you knew how. Many have tried, through transcendental meditation, and other, more 'scientific' means, such as hypnotism. They think they've covered a lot of ground, but all they've done is brush the dust off an unopened vault.

"There *is* a way to open that vault, and you find out how after I take you, but it can also be done *before* that time. It's actually very simple, *if you know how.*"

I sat back, my mind in total chaos. This meeting was *not* going the way I thought it would at all. Why was Death telling me all this? I'm an ad man, not a theologian. How was I to make all this sudden information work to change Death's image, make him "sellable"?

"Uh, everything you've told me is very… interesting, to put it mildly, but it seems to be an awful lot for the average consumer to, shall I say, 'buy into'. I think that most people in general are a bit uncomfortable with anything seriously pertaining to the supernatural, paranormal, metaphysical. Which is why, logically, they fear you.

"You want to change your image without spilling all your secrets, and I can understand this, but you may want to consider revealing one or two smaller ones, just to build the groundwork for trust, which is one of the positive steps you'll need. You say that death is just the natural conclusion to life, and I think all people know this in a basic way. Again, what they fear most is the *form* and *time* of your visits. Religion, for the most part, takes care in their minds what will happen to them after the fact, but few people have such a strong faith that they don't question this 'knowledge'. You may want to inform them that their consciousnesses will *not* end, their memories and personalities will remain intact..."

"Yes and no," Death interrupted, derailing my brain, which had been well into overdrive. "Everybody *does* change after death, it cannot be helped. A newborn baby is not the same creature as the fetus that had been floating in the womb for nine months. The same is true for a spirit newly liberated from the confines of the physical. A person's self-identity doesn't change, but just about everything else does..."

"And that's all a part of growing." My turn to interrupt, an idea starting to come to the fore of my mind. "That's what we'll base your PR campaign on. Personal growth. Death is just another step, like a child becoming an adult, but instead of physical, it's spiritual.

"You know, this may just affect how people act in general." I was starting to get excited. Idealism in the business world, what a concept. "You tell them that if they live their lives with compassion, generosity, and goodwill, this will make their continuing spiritual journey easier, allow them to grow and develop faster in the next phase of existence, while if they're selfish, greedy, malicious, and treat their fellow people like dirt, their personal growth will become stunted until they learn that their ways is nothing but a mistake, a cop-out, an unwillingness to take on self-responsibility that will only make their journey harder and longer. This could really work! If we market this right, people will actually look forward to your visit! Yes! What do you think?"

Death said nothing at first, just tapped a bony finger against the shaft of his scythe. "Mr. Cooper," he began. "Are you familiar with your Christian Bible?"

What? What the fuck was this? Didn't Death hear one word of this fantastic idea I just laid out for him? Granted, it certainly wasn't original. Religions have been preaching the same ideal for thousands of years. People wanted to believe it, but many couldn't bring themselves to do so. Unless, of course, the Source told them it was true. What better source, short of God, who didn't seem to care about his image, than Death himself, the doorman between existences?

Now he was bringing in the Bible? "A bit," I answered uncertainly.

"Matthew 7:3. Are you familiar with the verse?"

"No."

"Then let me enlighten you: *'And why do you look at the speck in your brother's eye, but do not consider the plank in your own eye?'*

"What have you done for your fellow human lately, Mr. Cooper? You talk a good idea, but to you it's just a way to make a ton of money. Just how much revenue did you expect me, and thereby yourself, to make on this venture? I'm not looking to merchandise myself. I'm not asking for something ludicrous like a line of 'Death-brand running shoes' or 'Grim Reaper action figures'. This isn't going to lead to a book deal and talk show appearances.

"I just want people to accept me; not resign themselves to me, *accept* me. That song and dance you just gave me sure sounded impressive, but it's already been tried. No one believes in the sincerity of it anymore, it's just Big Business now, the only concept they, and you, seem to be able to understand.

"The sad part is that you are closer to the truth than you realize within the simple confines of your marketing plan, but that's all it is to you, a marketing plan."

Oh, man. What a bunch of pretentious horseshit. *Death* came to *me* to be marketed, now he was giving me this Sunday morning evangelical sermon bullshit. Just what the fuck was going on here? I think Death was the one with the identity crisis. Just what the hell did he want from me, anyway?

"Look, Death, Mr. Reaper, whatever, what exactly are you looking to accomplish? What do you need from me?"

Death leaned forward. "What I need from you, Mr. Cooper, are all those despicable and foolish traits that almost all people seem to have, and of which you have made an earthly career. I need your greed, your materialism, your gloss and polish, your showmanship, your half-truths and subtle deceptions, your cynicism, your self-centeredness, and all the powers of persuasion and mind-control that are at your disposal. It is the sad truth that the grand majority of the people in this world will more readily believe what you have to tell them, even knowing that your sole intention is monetary gain, than they would believe the words of those very few who have a measure of genuine insight."

I leaned back, not trying very hard to suppress the triumphant smirk that was growing on my face. I no longer feared this apparition before me. Death needed my expertise! I had Death by the short hairs, and we both knew it. He knew that none of the Holy Rollers out there held any real credibility anymore. People knew, and believed, business. Business was practical, business was real, you knew it was by the money either going into or leaving your hands. And judging by the diplomas and award plaques on display on the wall behind me, along with my reputation, Death knew I was just the man to peddle his wares. So much for the mystery of the Great Beyond.

"Yes, of course," I said rather condescendingly. "It all comes down to that, doesn't it? Well, Mr. Reaper, you may not be interested in making a profit out of this, but I sure as hell am. I can provide what you require, but my services do not come inexpensively. The only question that remains is how you intend to pay for my despicable, money-grubbing skills. Just how did you intend to recompense me, Mr. Reaper?"

Death just stared at me with those vacant eye sockets. I was starting to get impatient with all this ominous bullshit when he finally spoke. "You will receive what so many others would pay very dearly for. It is something that no amount of money could ever buy."

Here we went again with this enigmatic crap. "And just what would that be?"

"A second chance."

At first I wasn't sure what Death had just said. A second chance? At what? Life? I was very happy with my life. I had a great career, financial success, three beautiful girlfriends who didn't care that the others existed as long as I kept them all in jewels and coke, a fantastic house out of town, two dynamite cars, and all the creature comforts that money could buy. What did I need a second chance at?

I'm sure Death didn't appreciate me laughing in his face, but I didn't give a shit. "What, are you offering to give me a conscience? Make me compassionate, generous, a boon to my fellow man? Make me want to give all my money to charities and live a life of self-contemplation and inner peace? Be like Scrooge at the end of *A Christmas Carol?* No thanks, Mr. Reaper, I like myself just the way I am: a pragmatic, greedy, materialistic asshole."

Death shook his hooded skull, which didn't surprise me. I knew he wasn't done trying to convince me.

"A child has a shiny rock and thinks he owns the entire world. A man has all that he can see, and thinks there is no more to receive. Limitations are reached yet are never acknowledged. What would you give to know your fate, Mr. Cooper?"

"What, do you mean am I going to be run over by a bus as soon as I walk out of this building tonight? Are you threatening me, Mr. Reaper?"

"No, the biggest threat to yourself lies from within you. It has never been your destiny for me to come for you. You will make the journey by your own act of will."

I was really beginning to get pissed off. "Just what the fuck are you talking about, Reaper? I haven't got all fucking night!"

"If you stay on this path, you haven't got ten more years."

"Spit it out! I'm sick of this bullshit!"

Death rose out of the chair, brandishing that wicked-looking scythe. My stomach sank as I realized I had pushed him too far. I held up my hands in supplication. The curved blade sliced through the empty space between us. I screamed in horror and closed my eyes, waiting for the metal to chop through my body.

174

It chopped through my mind instead. I found myself on the outside again, looking in, but instead of my body, I was seeing my true self, my inner self, cut open and presented for inspection.

What shocked me most was the emptiness. All of my supposed values, mercilessly exposed to the light of honest scrutiny, proved to be ephemeral, insubstantial. Where character was supposed to be were the ghostly shades of rationalization and denial. All my supposed successes and accomplishments were pale illusions that had the lifespan of a candle flickering out in an unstoppable breeze. There was nothing here that would be remembered or mourned when it passed on.

I saw my own realization of that in nine more years. I saw my despair as my life fell apart, my newfound self-knowledge making me act in ways that besmirched my reputation and destroyed all that I had striven for my entire life. I saw a bottle of vodka, and a .357 Magnum. I saw a pattern of brains and blood spattered all over the diplomas and award plaques behind my desk, the gun dropping from my lifeless hand, and the spectre of my present visitor coming to claim his prize, my spirit wailing in disconsolation and failure at life... too late...

"AAAAAAAAAAAH!"

I was back. Death sat before me, completely at ease. My breathing was harsh and ragged, but at least I was breathing.

"You owe me a service," came Death's calm voice.

I looked away, too shaken to reply.

"You believe now," Death continued. "But in a day it will all seem like a dream, a phantasm hallucinated due to stress and excess. You will take less and less credit in this prescience I have given you, and you will slip back into your old beliefs and habits, which is why I want a contract drawn up and signed *now*, while you're more… agreeable… to our deal. I'll even give you back your receptionist to write it up."

A sudden scream erupted from the outer office. My door burst open, and Dolores stood there, all color drained from her face, a dried trickle of blood around her ear. "Mr. Cooper! I…" she managed to exclaim before she saw my newest client. She screamed again, then collapsed to the floor in a dead faint.

"Then again, it looks like you'll have to get off your lazy ass and do it yourself."

"Yeah," I blurted out. "No problem. It doesn't need to be neatly printed with an impressive letterhead. Just let me get a paper and pen out of my desk." I rummaged around blindly, and remarkably came up with the items I needed.

"The first party, Carlton Edmund Cooper," I began to write and recite at the same time. "Do hereby agree to provide services for the second party, Mr. Grim Reaper, in contractual agreement for payment already received by the first party. Services are to include promotion of Mr. Reaper's statements and views concerning the legitimacy and naturalistic duties of his vocation, namely the eventual bringing of death to all members of the human race, through all the means of Mr. Cooper's disposal. Such promotions will meet with the approval of Mr. Reaper before they are enacted onto the public. Any problems or questions that may arise during the course of this arrangement will be satisfactorily settled by Mr. Cooper and Mr. Reaper before any further business is conducted… anything else, Mr. Reaper?"

"That is fine, Mr. Cooper. Please sign the document."

"Uh, you don't need my signature in blood, do you?

"Don't be ridiculous. Use the pen."

I signed the paper just as Dolores started to regain

consciousness. I slid the agreement over to Death, who perused the contract to make sure it stated what I said it stated before he applied his own signature. Dolores managed to stand on unsteady legs, keeping a fair distance from the dark figure. I gave her the arbitrary yet binding contract, and told her to make two copies of it. Still in shock, she just stood there, holding the paper limply. I yelled at her, and her natural subordination kicked in. She fled from my office. Death and I waited in uneasy silence until she returned with the copies.

I took one copy and handed over another to Death. "This is yours," I said stupidly, still feeling more than a little unreal. "And the original we'll give to a mutually chosen law firm to act as intermediary and judge in case a disagreement should surface. Agreed?"

"Yes, yes," Death said disinterestedly. "Give it to your own law firm if you so desire. I already know you'll abide by the terms in this contract. I have my way of enforcing your cooperation if you try to screw me, as I'm sure you now realize, and there isn't a lawyer you can hire who could bring any kind of lawsuit against me.

"I shall be in contact, Mr. Cooper, to monitor your progress." Death stood up, shouldering that awful scythe. "One last thing. Try not to forget your experiences here tonight. They will seem more illusory as time goes by, but they are the truth, and if you look deep enough inside yourself, you will see that this is so. You may want to consider giving up the booze and the drugs and getting rid of that handgun you purchased for your 'personal protection'." Death turned around and walked out the door.

I looked at my gold and diamond watch. It was 7:00 p.m. on a Friday evening. I knew nothing more would be accomplished until Monday morning, and that I had an entire weekend to relive this terrible hour over and over. I looked at the contract. It stayed corporeal, and so did Death's signature. I had one hell of a job to accomplish, and a lot of planning and brainstorming to do.

I looked up at Dolores, who was still standing there speechless. "You can leave now, Dolores. Have a nice weekend." She just stood there. I repeated myself more forcibly. She slowly and silently walked out. I knew she would never return. I made a mental note to put out an ad for a new receptionist.

Where to start? Probably ads in various newspapers and magazines, maybe in scientific journals. Stay away from credibility-destroying occult publications. Recruit some convincing spokespeople, no Bible-thumpers or any other religious yo-yos, no fortune-telling, tarot-card dealing New Age weirdos, nothing that most people would laugh at, maybe some renowned scientists, especially if Death was willing to personally visit and convince them as he had done me. After practical credibility had been established, then maybe some genuinely respected spiritual leaders could come into the picture, depending on Death's discretion, of course.

Was Death right? Would I eventually revert back to my former gluttonous self? I didn't honestly know. It was all so convincing now, with Death's presence still palpable in this office, but would it be so come a bright Monday morning? I turned in my chair and looked at my back wall, adorned with memorabilia. I remembered the crimson spray that I had seen drip from it, *will* drip from it, if I chose to forget what happened here tonight.

If nothing else, the gun had to go. Maybe that vial of snort I had in my car could go, too. I touched the back of my head, feeling the balding crown I so hated. But at least it was intact, not a gaping hole. I realized that there were much more important things to lose than hair. Maybe a slight change wouldn't hurt, after all. Fuck it, my life had too much stress in it as it was. I really wasn't enjoying myself anymore. After this job was completed, maybe it would be time to think things through.

Then I remembered my ladies, and I felt a twinge in my groin. I had plenty of time to think about this shit Monday.

Odds 'n Ends: Five Micro Stories for the Price of One

1. Mazu's Gift

The girl was twelve years old and dressed in old, worn garments given to her by compassionate souls. She had nothing else except her name, Gaiyu.

A full moon rode through the heavens, illuminating the ocean. Gaiyu had paid the temple priest with the last of her dead mother's money to perform the invocation. All she could do now was stand and wait.

A wave crashed on the shore, its foam building and taking the shape of a young woman. The water receded, leaving the goddess, dressed in red, standing before Gaiyu. The girl knelt and lowered her eyes.

What is it you wish? The goddess asked.

Gaiyu looked up. "I seek vengeance, beautiful Mazu, upon the man who killed my mother."

Why did this man kill your mother?

Tears fell from the girl's eyes. "My mother was a prostitute. The man is a sailor, and he killed her after he had his way with her. I would see him punished."

The goddess glowed in the moonlight. *What do you offer?*

The girl swallowed. "I have nothing to offer but myself."

It is enough.

A funnel of sea water engulfed Gaiyu. She did not resist the heavy coldness that filled her lungs. Gaiyu's consciousness floated from her dead body.

Behold your new home.

Gaiyu flexed her powerful, scaled neck and shot through the water. Ahead lay the ship with the *laowai* sailor, a puny construction of wood and rope. She rose, glittering with fire and blood, and the sailor who killed her mother roasted on her fangs.

2. Gabriel Ratchets

The moon painted its pale light across crooked trees and darkened homes. Somewhere behind it, the Gabriel Ratchets bayed in the excitement of the Hunt.

The blood on Colin's hands glistened black. He cursed the girl who had forced him to kill her. She'd been beautiful, fifteen years old at the most. All he had wanted was a kiss, and maybe a bit of hand warming. But the girl had struggled and yelled for help. Colin had panicked and picked up a rock and...

And now the Gabriel Ratchets were after him.

Colin knew they watched over certain villages. It was just his luck he had wandered into one of them. Why couldn't the girl have just done what he wanted? Was a little affection too much to ask for?

He looked up at the moon. Dark shapes, fierce and hungry, tore their way toward him from the amber light. Colin cried and broke into a run.

Heavy paws hit the earth behind him. Colin glanced back. The hounds were monstrous, with thick black fur and burning eyes. Saliva flew back from drawn muzzles. Teeth, long and terrible, snapped in the lunar light.

They growled in satisfaction; their quarry would not escape.

Colin screamed as canine fangs sank into the flesh of his thigh. The pack bore him down.

Within minutes, blood and gnawed bone were all that remained. Sated howls rose to the red-limned sky.

3. Hostile Takeover the Banshee Way

The wailing tore through me. I wanted nothing more than to lie down.

But I did not become the CEO for Goliath Tech by lying down. I did it by forcing my predecessor out, despite the Board's objections. I strode across the vast lawn of my summer home to the stream that ran along its western edge, a member of my security team by my side. Whoever was making this racket would be facing serious trespassing charges.

From the back she looked old, with long, white hair that hung nearly to the ground. Her clothes were in tatters, and she appeared to be washing something at the stream's edge. I yelled out to her and she turned.

She was hideous. Her eyes were red, her nose long and bent, and when she opened her mouth her teeth were long and black. I paused. The security guard stiffened and reached for his gun. I held out a hand to restrain him.

Then I noticed what she was washing.

It was one of my best suits, a basalt blue Ermenegildo Zegna worth $8000. Now it was ruined.

"What the hell are you doing?" I demanded.

"Your time is nigh," she screeched at me. "See, you have brought your doom!"

Enough was enough. I turned to the guard. "Take this woman and contact the police."

I looked in shock at the gun pointed at my head. "Sorry, boss, but the Board has decided you need to be replaced."

4. The Hottest Girls Around

"You'll love this place. It's loaded with the hottest chicks anywhere!"

I had him. Girls were the honey that Shaun could not resist.

I'm an imp, the real deal, straight from Hell. But I don't look it. I look like any other human. It would be hard to get things done if I wore my natural shape. I'd stick out.

The funny part? Shaun knows I'm an imp. Part of the deal is that I don't keep that a secret. Yet he still follows me wherever I lead. A classic case of the little head doing the thinking for the big head. No shortage of those types of guys.

"What's the name of this place?" he asked.

"Club Gehenna."

"Cool name. Sounds sinful!"

"It is." I assured him.

We turned down an alley stinking of piss and decomposing trash. It came to a dead-end at a brick wall.

I turned to Shaun. "Have you come by your own free will?"

Shaun looked for an entrance. "Yeah, sure," he said absentmindedly.

That's all I needed. I knocked once on the wall.

The bricks peeled back. A blast of brimstone washed over us.

Two gorgeous women appeared at Shaun's side. Each took one of his hands. Their touch burned his flesh down to the bone.

Shawn screamed as they dragged him into the opening.

"You wanted the hottest chicks!" I yelled at him as he disappeared into darkness. "You got 'em!"

My reward was another year to walk the earth.

5. Such A Precocious Child

"Lauren, what have you done?"

Dr. Lauren Mehra held her wife's hands. "Jo, our daughter will never be sick. And she'll be incredibly intelligent."

Jo pulled her hands away. "Lauren, I agreed to being implanted with a fertilized egg. I did not agree to what you did to it!"

"All I did was make our child better. Eugenics is fast becoming a respectable science. We need to be at the forefront."

"Lauren…"

"Think about it, Jo! Our daughter will be the progenitor of humanity's future. We'll be…"

"She talks to me, Lauren."

Lauren paused, mouth open.

"She tells me things," Jo continued. "Scary things. Terrible things."

"Impossible!" Lauren said. "This is only the 20th week. The baby cannot possibly be cognizant or able to communicate."

Tears spilled from Jo's pale blue eyes. "Listen to me, Lauren. She talks to me, through my mind. And don't tell me that I'm experiencing some sort of prepartum psychosis! This is real!"

Lauren shook her head. "I know you think this is real, but I assure you it's not. I think we need to run some tests, see what's going on."

Jo's head jerked back, and she gasped for breath.

"Jo, what is it?"

Jo's eyes found Lauren's. "She's taking over. My God..."

"Jo!"

Jo's features relaxed. She looked at Lauren with eyes that held a dark intelligence.

"Hello, Mother," her daughter said. "I have plans, and you will assist. Disobedience will be dealt with harshly."

A big "thank you" goes out to my family, who has never stopped believing in me, and to my friends, who are always there to help me up when I stumble. My appreciation is profound.

About the Author

Paul Magnan has been writing stories that veer from the straight and narrow for many years. He lives in the wilds of Rhode Island with his family.

Made in the USA
Middletown, DE
09 September 2022